SHE LIVES IN MY LAP

Image used courtesy of CreateHerStock.com

ISBN: 9781020001116

45 Alternate Press, LLC
Hampton, VA

SHE LIVES IN MY LAP

A NOVELLA

RAN WALKER

In Memory of
Elizabeth "Meatmumma" Stokes

ONE

In retrospect, I really should have seen it coming, but I had no idea that my father would hit me with it before I could take off my suit and change into something more comfortable, like the t-shirt and shorts in my backpack beside the hotel door. Instead of the congratulatory dinner at some swanky restaurant in downtown Atlanta, I got "the speech," no less than three hours after accepting my hard-earned Bachelor of Arts degree from Ellison-Wright College.

As my father would have been quick to point out, that was my problem: I didn't seem to take him seriously when he established ultimatums. I figured it was all just tough talk and that he would save the heavy stuff for me after I had folded up my graduation robe and put it away.

I was wrong.

"Don't I get a grace period or something? Like six months to get on my feet?" I asked, floored by my father's latest announcement.

He looked at me with as straight a face as I had ever seen. "You should've been looking for a job this past semester."

"But I was studying."

"Really?" he asked, his voice heavy with sarcasm. "We spent over $140,000 over the last six years putting you through college. You changed majors three times and still graduated with only a 2.3. Your mother and I promised you we'd pay for college, and we did. Now you have officially graduated out of my wallet. You're on your own."

"What does that mean? Are you kicking me out of the house?"

"No—but you'll be paying rent from here on out, that is if you want to stay with us."

"Rent? For my own room?"

He nodded, his eyes unflinching.

"How much?" It was all I could think to ask.

"$500."

"$500 for my room?"

"Yes."

"Mom!" I pleaded, looking in her direction.

She looked away, unable to meet my eyes. I knew she had cosigned on my father's decision.

"Where am I supposed to get $500 from?"

"Where do you think? Get a job."

"Doing what?"

"Who knows? You could pick cotton for all I care. I just want my rent money on the first of each month."

I sat down on the bed in my parents' Ritz Carlton hotel room. Everything was going so fast. I already had plans to hit up a few parties with some of my boys later on that night. Now I was trying to digest what my father was laying on me.

"Dad, for $500 I could just get an apartment here in Atlanta and find a roommate. I know the cost of living has to be much lower in Mississippi."

"Boy, is that the best you can do in the way of negotiating?"

Not realizing that I was doing just that, I reluctantly nodded.

"Shit. $140,000 and my boy can't even negotiate."

"Well, I'm not a judge like you," I responded, a little too smartly, but looked to soften it by adding, "I have been thinking about law school though."

"Apparently not enough. You haven't even taken the LSAT. With your GPA you'd be fighting uphill the whole way, and as of now, your mother and I are no longer responsible for footing the bill."

I lowered my elbows onto my thighs and rested my head in my hands. I can't say that I felt on the verge of tears, but I was more than a little taken aback.

"Couldn't all of this have waited until I at least had a day to savor my degree?"

My mother walked up next to me and placed her hand on my shoulder. "We're leaving out tomorrow, headed back to Mississippi."

"What does that mean?"

My father rested his hand on top of the dresser facing the bed. "It means that you have a few hours to make up your mind about what you want to do. If you come with us, I'll give you a month before I start charging you. If you stay here, you're on your own."

"When do I have to let you know something?"

"We leave out at ten in the morning."

Excusing myself, I darted out of the hotel and down Peachtree Street. I could hardly think, but I knew I couldn't put off making this decision. Not like the other times. My father was serious, and for a moment, I was envious of my little sister who was on track to becoming a member of the Phi Beta Kappa chapter at Princeton. Her summer internship had prevented her from coming down for my graduation, but I was actually relieved that she hadn't been around to see her big bro get the boot from Dad.

I pulled my cell phone from my pocket and started placing calls. With any luck, I could create a few options for myself. The only problem was that I didn't really know what I wanted to do. And to my father, that was the $140,000 question that I could no longer afford to ask.

EVEN WHILE I was still attending Daily High School, the only high school in my hometown of fifteen thousand people, my father and I had had philosophical battles over whether or not I was just an average student or if I was a lazy kid who was actually gifted in some way. Leading up to my senior year in high school, I was convinced that I was winning the war when, out of the blue, my ACT scores arrived at the mailbox down the driveway from our large, brick two level house outside of the city limits, or, as my classmates would say, out in the boondocks. I thought the "30" listed as my cumulative score was a typo. When I showed it to my father, he beamed with happiness.

"Now you'll get a scholarship," he said, raising my scores to the ceiling with both hands, as if he were Rafiki holding baby Simba before hundreds of bowing zebras and giraffes.

My GPA in high school wasn't terribly impressive at a 2.6, but Ellison-Wright College, a small, but prestigious Historically Black College in Atlanta, was willing to overlook that due to my test score and the fact that I had been a tuba player in the marching band for four years (just long enough to realize that I didn't want to walk around a football field in all that heat with a hulking mass of metal wrapped around my shoulder). But it qualified as an extracurricular activity, and since I was a pretty decent writer of personal essays who had a fairly high test score, that was all it took to seal the deal.

The school also fit the unwritten requirements my father had for the type of school I should attend. In his Buppie world of doctors, lawyers, engineers, and businessmen, I had to attend a school with a reputation. Yes, Judge Norman Davis's son had to go to a school that people in Daily, Mississippi, had heard of, especially since it was out of state. Of course the only people who would have even known about Ellison-Wright were people in the aforementioned group of black professionals. Most of the white people in Daily had never heard of Ellison-Wright, let alone any Historically Black College.

My father and mother had gone to Morehouse and Spelman, respectively, so I grew up going to homecoming games and Founder's Days every other year, socializing and hobnobbing with the children of my parents' classmates. It wasn't a bad thing; in fact, it was actually a lot of fun. When we'd get back to Daily, however, it didn't take long before I was reminded that you could drive an eighteen-wheeler through the distance between the way black people were perceived in Mississippi versus the way they were perceived in Atlanta. So when I got the acceptance letter from Ellison-Wright, my parents were excited. I would be in Atlanta, and as far as they were concerned, that was the place for a kid like me. I'd realize my potential there, my father hoped. Then I'd graduate, get a great job, and get a straw Alumni hat to wear at the homecoming games when we played Morehouse or Clark Atlanta. I'd taunt my father in jest, and he'd do the same; then we'd smoke cigars and talk about creating a family dynasty like the Rockefellers or Vanderbilts.

But my experience at Ellison-Wright was nothing like that. I started with a major in biology, before failing the only (and intro level) biology class I was taking. By the end of my first semester, I had lost my scholarship, so I switched my major to business and did a full year there before I realized that I didn't have the discipline or interest in going to a corporate job everyday, wearing a suit and tie. I actually ended up majoring in English, more as a last resort, simply because I enjoyed reading and writing. Plus, my father felt I'd be in a decent position to either teach or go to law school. After six years, though, he was more concerned about me getting a degree than he was anything else. I took this to mean that he wanted me to pursue my dreams and be happy with my life, but a few hours after the graduation ceremony, I realized that he had just given up on me.

Now I was walking aimlessly down Peachtree Street, flipping through my phone and dialing numbers. I called guys who'd finished two years earlier (in what should have been my graduating class). I called guys who I'd just graduated with (although most of them were off somewhere partying or spending time with their families). I even called a few female friends (those who were purely platonic and even a few who'd been "buddies" every once in a while). Nothing. Nada. I almost gave up when I reluctantly called a local guy named McCarthy, who was famous for hanging out with college students and seemed to have an endless stack of video games and junk food. His crib in Southwest Atlanta was like Neverland Ranch for college slackers. I'd been over there three years in a row for

Super Bowl parties and with only hours to give my father a decision, I called him.

"Speak, nigga," McCarthy said answering his cell phone.

"This is Lincoln?"

"Naw, nigga. Lincoln is dead."

"Not that Lincoln. The one from Ellison-Wright."

"You roll up with me?"

"What? Naw, man. I went to a few of your parties and stuff."

"For real? Who yo peeps?"

"Mugsy, Frank, Teddy, you know. Guys from Ellison-Wright."

He laughed. "Yeah, a'ight. What's up? You looking to blaze up?"

"Nah. I'm looking for a place to crash for a few days while I look for an apartment."

"For real? Why you callin' *me?*"

He was right. Why in the hell *was* I calling him? "Desperation" didn't seem like the appropriate answer though. I didn't have any idea of what I wanted to say, but it didn't stop me from trying.

"Do you know anybody who might let me crash on a couch for a few days?"

"Hmmm," he responded, as if going into deep thought. "How much you got?"

"Man, I just finished school. I don't even have a job yet."

"So you lookin' for the free-ninety-nine thing?"

"Something like that."

He laughed in my ear—and it wasn't even the polite kind of chuckle you'd expect from a person who cared about the feelings of the person he was talking to. He let loose as if I were Kevin Hart doing an encore. I almost hung up on him.

When he could finally calm himself down long enough to speak, he said, "I ain't got no bed for you, but if you just looking to sleep somewhere for a few days, you can lay out on the floor or something. Just don't get in the way."

"Man, thank you!" I said. I didn't know if I would even take him up on his offer, but at least I had something to compare to my father's ultimatum. "I'll holler at you tomorrow then."

"A'ight. Just a few days, and this ain't no cell block. Ain't no three hots and a cot. Just the floor."

"Got you," I said.

I hung up my cell phone and looked up to see where I was. I couldn't believe that I had reached Buckhead already. My feet were killing me. I could literally feel my feet swelling inside of my shoes as I stood there.

I felt around in my pocket for a few dollars and hailed a cab back to the Ritz Carlton. When I entered the lobby, I decided to camp out downstairs while I considered what I would tell my father. Crashing with McCarthy was hardly a plan, but it would buy me time to check with my friends tomorrow and see about something a bit more stable—or at the very least something that included a bed. The alternative was to suck up my pride and head back to Daily with my parents. When I thought about the comfort of living at home and eating home-cooked meals, I was tempted. My father hadn't said anything about my having to pay for meals. Plus, my mother would've probably drawn the line there. She loved to cook, and she loved to watch us eat the experiments that she prepared from the downloaded recipes on the Food Network website.

Still, there was the issue of the money. Daily was small. Too small. And my father knew that. He knew I had outgrown it. He also knew that Daily was more of a factory town and that I would have difficulty getting a job there. The only job I could think of that I was qualified on some level to attempt by the fall was teaching. And I wasn't even certified for that. I'd be substitute teaching, scraping by to get rent. In Atlanta, I would have a lot more opportunities to pursue. I'd also have friends around me who understood my plight. Walking to the elevator, I knew it wouldn't be as easy a decision as I had originally thought.

As soon as I reached the room, I slid off my shoes and lay down on the couch in the den. I could hear them snoring loudly in the bedroom.

I fixed my eyes on the ceiling, unable to make out anything in the darkness of the room. I hoped that I would have an epiphany, but I didn't. In fact, I drifted off to sleep with the odd feeling of a giant question mark resting upon my chest.

I WOKE to the smell of my father's dark, spicy cologne hovering in the air and the sound of my mother pressing off steam from the hotel iron. I immediately looked at my watch, realizing that I had two hours before my parents departed.

"We're about to go get breakfast. If you want to go, you'll need to be ready in the next fifteen minutes," my mother said, resting the iron on the board and handing my father his maroon colored polo shirt.

I stumbled from the couch and saw my father sitting on the edge of the bed, remote control in hand, eyes fixed on CNN.

"Good morning, Dad," I offered.

"Good morning, Link!" he responded, as if he were

born to take on the day. "We're headed down to get breakfast in a few. You coming?"

"That's the plan," I said. "Just about to hop in the shower."

"Okay. We're leaving out in fifteen minutes."

"Yeah, that's what Mom just said. I'll be out in a minute."

As I rotated myself quickly beneath the steaming water of the shower, I realized that I didn't *hate* my father or anything close to it. We just had different approaches to life. He was used to being in control of things, and I was enjoying the lifestyle of not having anyone to tell me what to do. The only question was whether or not I was ready to step out from under my father's wings and taste life without a safety net. Dad was already cutting the strings, so the question that really lingered was whether or not I would allow him to control me after he had cut them.

As soon as my foot touched the cool floor in front of the tub and I reached for my towel, I knew I had just taken my official first step toward independence. I knew I would have breakfast with my family and tell them afterwards that I was staying. I knew my father would hug me, slapping me on my back, and tell me that I was now officially an adult. I also knew my mother would tear up a little. But I didn't know how I would feel watching their BMW pulling away from the curb of the Ritz Carlton.

Part of me felt as though I might have been drawing my line in the sand far too soon, but the other part of me felt that I was about to undertake an adventure, the likes of which I had never experienced before in my life. But wasn't that the whole point of graduating from college? Experience new things, make a life for yourself? That was what I was going to do.

The success story of my life would start with the direction of my feet, which, at the moment, were pointed toward Southwest Atlanta and the floor of a guy who seemed like the most questionable of people to begin such a journey. But every journey had to start somewhere, and that's where mine would start.

TWO

Much of the tone of my relationship with McCarthy was set when he came to the door of his apartment to let me in. Dressed in a wife-beater and boxers with his junk falling out of the slit in the front, he struck me as completely oblivious to even the most basic of details. I didn't bother saying anything about his junk. Instead, I just thanked him for giving me a place to crash.

"Don't get too comfortable. Think of this place like a revolving door. You just walking your way right through."

"Well, thanks anyway."

"I'm just sayin'. I had this dude last year who was here so long the nigga was getting mail. And he had a job, too! Just trifling-ass folks, know what I'm sayin'?"

"No doubt." There was no way I would let myself sleep on this dude's floor any longer than I had to. "A few days—just until I can get my stuff lined up."

"A'ight," McCarthy said. "One thing, though. You ain't 5-0, are you? You have to tell a nigga if you are."

"No. I just graduated from school," I responded. "What, are they hiring?"

It was supposed to be a joke, but McCarthy just

shrugged. "You should just do that MMA stuff if you wanna whip a nigga's ass, man."

I couldn't tell if he was joking or not, so I nodded and lugged my suitcase and backpack over to the wall in the den.

I was able to negotiate with my father to pay for storage so I could keep my stuff here in Atlanta, but it didn't come without strings attached. He would only pay for three months, and at the end of six months, I had to pay him back for his three. He almost charged me interest, but decided against it at the last minute. "Part of my graduation gift to you," he had said.

The apartment was a small one-bedroom over in West End, but it was less than a block from the MARTA train station.

"Mac, your dick is hanging out again," said a woman who had been sitting in the den, but whom I had failed to notice until that moment.

"My bad," he said, stretching out his waistband and pulling his junk through the slit, like a sailor hoisting an anchor up from the depths of the ocean.

"Paris," the woman said, holding out her hand to me.

"Lincoln," I said, reluctantly shaking it. For all I knew, she might have had her hand on McCarthy before I arrived.

"He's dead," she said, laughing.

"That's what I keep hearing."

Paris was the kind of woman who could blend into the background, but emerge like one of those 3D book images if you were facing her directly. She was actually rather striking, her twists, almost like dreadlocks, pulled away from her face into a ponytail. I fell in love for two seconds, until I heard McCarthy sit back on his recliner and lift his feet up. It wasn't good etiquette to check out another dude's woman, especially if he was giving you a place to crash. I found a free spot on the empty, adjacent love seat.

"You smoke?" Paris asked, holding a vaporizer to her lips and taking in a little.

"Naw. I'm good."

Paris rose from the couch and walked over to McCarthy to give him a hit. Once he finished, she walked back to her seat, my eyes following her the entire time.

"I don't know how you do it?" McCarthy said.

"What?" I asked.

"Not you, nigga. P, how you keep walking back and forth with that kush like that. Most niggas would be on they backs right now. That's some potent shit."

Paris chuckled to herself. "This is nice stuff, but I didn't just wake up this morning and start smoking."

We sat for a while staring at old game shows on that game show channel. By ten o'clock, I decided that I needed to get off my ass and go and try to find some work somewhere. I would hit up at least one place before lunch. As I considered where I might eat, I decided to make it a fast food place where I wouldn't have to tip anybody. I wanted the small stack in my savings to last me for a while, just in case it took me a while to get on my feet.

"Well, I'm about to head out for a bit," I said, rising from the couch. "Do I need a key or something?"

"Nah," McCarthy said. "Just call before you come back. I'll make sure someone's here to let you in."

"Okay. Cool."

Just as I headed toward the door, Paris stood up. "Yo, hold up. I'm about to head out, too."

She walked over and gave McCarthy a pound before following me out the door.

As we walked across the street to the MARTA station, I asked, "How long have you been with McCarthy?"

"Mac? Not even. That's my boy. I smoke out with him sometimes, but it ain't like *that*. Eww," she said. "You see how ashy that nigga's dick was?"

I laughed so hard that I almost rolled onto the sidewalk. "I was trying not to look."

"He definitely ain't my type," she said, laughing.

"So which way are you headed?" I asked.

"I'm thinking about getting something to eat," she said, pulling a small toothbrush from her purse and placing it in her mouth.

"Well, I think I'm going to head up to Lenox."

"I can do that. You wanna grab a bite at the food court?"

"Sure," I responded, still trying to figure out what lottery I had won to have her company.

Once we got onto the train, I had to break down and ask her about the toothbrush.

"I use it to massage my gums after I smoke. It keeps me from eating too much junk food."

"I don't think I've ever heard of that before."

"Well, you don't smoke, so why would you?" she said, smiling.

"True."

"So you just finished school? That's what Mac said."

"Yeah. A degree in English from Ellison-Wright."

"Nice," she said, putting the toothbrush back into its case in her purse. "What do you plan to do with that?"

"I'm still trying to figure that out. At this point, I will do just about anything to get some income coming in."

"Don't say anything. You should have some standards."

"Well, I didn't mean it *literally*."

"Young brother, we are our words, so be careful how you use them. You put shit out into the universe, you get shit right back."

I nodded, assuming this was just the weed talking.

"So can I ask you a question?" I said.

"Was *that* the question? Or is there another one?"

Touché. "Okay. You said earlier that Mac wasn't your type."

"And your question is what?"

"What *is* your type?"

She smiled. "You trying to holler, or is this just pure curiosity?"

"I guess a bit of both."

She smiled. "I like interesting people. If you have an open heart and we vibe, I'll at least give you the benefit of the doubt."

"Am I interesting?"

"I don't know. Are you?"

"I guess you'll have to tell me once you get to know me."

"Okay," she responded, patting my leg.

As the train continued racing along the tracks, my mind raced with it. I had no idea of how old Paris was, what she did for a living, whether there was someone special in her life, or whether I was over-thinking this thing. The only real answer I could arrive at by the time we exited the train at Lenox was that I was definitely over-thinking everything. Yesterday I had no idea of what today would hold. I had already decided to give myself over to the adventure of it all, and well, this was a part of that adventure.

"SO WHAT DO YOU DO?" I asked, as we sat down near the Chinese food restaurant I had bought our food from. While it forced me to recalculate my budget, I had no intention of not paying for her meal. Even if she had added herself to the equation without my invitation.

"I write."

"Books? Articles?"

"I'm a poet—but I'm working on a novel."

"Does poetry pay well?"

"Ha," she said, lifting her head to let out a laugh that was far more melodious than I would have ever anticipated. "I like that you added the word 'well' to that question. If it pays at all, it keeps losing my address to send me my check."

"Well, how do you pay your bills?"

"All kinds of ways. Mainly I work at a consignment shop over in Little Five Points, but I also do a little modeling and occasionally I'll sit for an art class, sing the hook on a rap track, or maybe even flip something on Ebay. I like trying new things."

This girl was the quintessential hustler. But if she was paying rent and supporting a weed habit, she had to keep some plates in the air. I wondered if I was looking at the female version of who I would become.

"Wow. You're pretty busy. I'm surprised you're not working today."

"I'll be working later. It's all good."

"Doin' the most, I guess."

She laughed again, before swirling some lo mein onto her plastic fork and placing it into her mouth.

"So what do you have going on later?" I asked.

"Stuff."

"Sorry. I didn't mean to get too far up in your Kool-Aid."

"It's all right. But trust me. I'm good for later."

We sat finishing our meal. The food court was full from the lunch crowd, people who had jobs. All I had to do was find something to get a paycheck coming in. It didn't have to be a career. A job would suffice. Glancing around the food court, I figured I could easily find a job somewhere in the mall, maybe a sneaker store or something.

"Hey, thanks for lunch," Paris said. "I just didn't want you to think I was the kind of sista who didn't say thank you."

"Hey, no problem. I'm glad to have your company."

"Why do you say that?"

"You're dope—and mysterious. I guess I like that combination."

"Mysterious? Haven't heard that one before, but hey, I'll take it." She took a sip of her soda and pushed her empty plate to the side. "So can I ask you a question?"

"Sure."

"What's your deal? You look like the kind of guy who comes from money. You got a good degree from a good school. Why the hell are you crashing at Mac's crib? You call me a mystery, but for real, you're the mystery."

"I guess I didn't plan what I would do after I graduated from college too well."

She laughed. "Did you plan it at all?"

I laughed along with her. "I don't know. Maybe not enough."

"Well, you get no judgement from me. My shit is

so all over the place. I'm in no position to wonder how you blew your lead on the rest of society."

"Damn. Nice backhanded compliment."

"You know what I mean."

"Yeah. I'm just out here in the world trying to get my game plan in order," I said.

"Well, good luck with that shit, Lincoln."

"Hey, I know you have to work this evening, but if you're free later, maybe we could hang out."

Paris stood up and grabbed her empty plate and cup. "I like you," she said. "But you're kind of thirsty, aren't you?"

"Damn," I responded. "My face is on the floor."

"Go handle your business. Get that job. I'm sure our paths'll cross again."

"Well, all right then," I responded, not knowing what else to say.

"A'ight," she said. "Peace."

And like that, she walked away, leaving me at the table with remnants of my lo mein staring back at me from a greasy foam plate.

THREE

I sat at the table for another ten minutes, reflecting over my conversation with Paris. I couldn't really tell if I had been dissed or playfully joned. But more than anything, I was disappointed with myself for even caring that much in the first place. Clearly she was right about the job thing, even if I didn't want to admit it.

I stood up from the table and walked over to the escalator. One of the good things about getting a part-time job at a place like the mall was that I could still keep looking for something bigger during my off time. No one expected me to be at a part-time job forever. The turnover rate at a mall job demanded that I find something better eventually, I figured.

As I started walking around asking for applications, I realized that I had seriously overestimated my ability to get a job. With the summer coming for everyone, just about every sixteen-year-old in Fulton County had already beaten me to the punch. One manager at a department store told me flat-out that I was over qualified for the kind of jobs they had open at the moment. I wondered how that could be when I had never had a job.

From Lenox Mall I walked to Phipps Plaza. The results were the same. After I hit up a few more stores and needlessly filled out a few more applications, I was starting to think that maybe the universe was conspiring against me. Either that, or I had simply went to all of the wrong spots on the first day of my job hunt.

By the time I made it back to McCarthy's place, I had already decided to work my job search like the rest of the people of my generation: use my fucking phone.

While I could've grabbed dinner somewhere, I wanted desperately to get back on budget. Plus, I had had a late lunch. I didn't need to eat again for the rest of the day. I was good. It wasn't like I was starving. I read somewhere that when Richard Wright was growing up, he used to go to sleep to avoid being hungry. I doubted it would ever come to that for me, but if it did, I would just sleep through my hunger. At the end of the day, I wasn't going to starve, so my situation was just a first world problem anyway.

As I lay on some blankets against the back wall of the den and charged my phone, I wondered how much longer my father and mother would carry me on their phone plan. We hadn't discussed that, and since there were no guarantees I would have unlimited data going forward, I would need to seek out free Wi-Fi access from somewhere. A McDonald's or a bookstore maybe. Even though I was fairly familiar with the neighborhood, I had no ready answer available. Maybe there was a public library nearby. My Ellison-Wright password probably still worked, too.

Then it hit me! I wouldn't blow another day walking around to stores. If I was going to do something beyond the Internet, it would be to go over to the Career Placement office on campus. Hell, that's what the office was for: helping people like me who didn't quite figure out the next step in enough time to make a smooth transition from graduation into the real world.

With my plan fixed firmly in place, I closed my eyes and told myself that I wasn't hungry.

I WOKE up early and grabbed a shower before Mc-Carthy could get up. The entire house smelled like beer, weed, and ass. I mentally added another thing to my list of things to do that day: call around and see if I might be able to crash at any of my other boys' cribs. Surely someone was still in town. Hell, we just graduated, and I knew someone had to have a lease running through to the end of the month. I had options. I had to. Camping out on a McCarthy's floor wasn't a plan. It was me giving up, and I decided I wasn't going to do that anymore.

The campus was close enough to West End to walk to, so I started walking in that direction. The office opened at 8:30 a.m., and I figured I would be there as soon as the doors opened.

My stomach grumbled as I walked. Still a few blocks from campus, I looked around to see what my food options were. Most of them were fast food restaurants that specialized in greasy breakfast combos. As hungry as I was, I wasn't sure if something like that would actually upset my stomach, so I looked around for grocery stores or really any place that sold fruit. I had never been the "fruit for breakfast" type, but I was now a graduate, so now was as good a time as any to try to start taking better care of myself. That was also one of the reasons I was walking as many places as I could. My old rust bucket Mercedes was guzzling gas and spitting up oil like it was part college frat boy, part newborn baby. That's the reason I preferred to take the train: with maintenance and gas, it was just cheaper.

The only grocery store in the area was a Keno's, which was a hood grocery store where the only thing fresh in there was the stank attitude of the employee at the check-out counter. The bananas looked like plantains, and the apples looked like plums. There was usually some kind of insect flying around the produce area, and they always seemed to have sales on massive jugs of fruit drinks that contained no actual fruit. They didn't even sell energy bars. Still, I walked around in the store, hoping to find something that I may have once overlooked or dismissed in the past.

After a few minutes, my stomach was begging me for sustenance, so I bought a bag of salt and vinegar potato chips and a soda. One of my boys once told me the rules of eating: (1) eat, and (2) if you can eat well, do so. In this situation I was lucky to eat, so I was just going to go with that for now.

I continued down the street eating chips and drinking soda as I approached the campus. I headed straight for the Career Placement office building and found the first restroom I could so that I could piss away the soda that had already begun to run through me and wash all of the chip seasonings off my hands. I looked at myself in the mirror. I was the same dude who was just enrolled a few days ago. Not much had changed in the last few days, except for my father and mother giving me that ultimatum to leave or stay. If there was anything else I was seeing in the mirror, it was the product of my imagination.

I couldn't for the life of me think of any of the names of the people working in Career Placement. I had guessed I would never really need to use their services. How could I have allowed myself to not do anything to prepare for post-graduation? It wasn't like I was that busy. I guessed I just thought that was what the summer was for. Deep down (or not so deep down) I had imagined that I could just move out of my dorm and into a place in midtown, where I could casually do my job search. In fact, in my mind I would have been on a vacation, celebrating my degree, before I came back to do anything remotely related to finding employment.

My vacation had turned into trying to get a job, and the second stop on my trip was the Career Placement office. I sat by the door, glancing at my watch and scanning over my resume, which was saved in an app on my phone. When the door opened at 8:30, I eagerly arose from my seat and walked in.

"Can I help you?" the receptionist asked, briefly taking a sip from her mug of coffee.

"Yes. I'd like to meet with one of your counselors about doing a job search. I just graduated."

"Oh, congratulations!" she said, smiling heartily. "Have you been here before?"

"No, ma'am. This is my first time."

"Well, that's all right. We will take care of you. Just have a seat over there," she said, pointing to a small row of chairs just off from the entrance door.

As I sat down, I could feel a mega-ton weight being lifted from my shoulders. Today would be the day that I was going to find a job.

Late last night while trying to fall asleep, I considered what kind of jobs I would be interested in. The list I came up with included publishing, entertainment (TV, film, or music), sports, and maybe something dealing with law that didn't require me to be a lawyer. I was ready for my meeting. I just needed someone from

Ellison-Wright to help me grease open the door. Surely they could do that. After $140,000, that was the least they could do, I figured.

"Good morning," said a tall guy who looked a lot like Idris Elba. "I'm Frank Dole."

I stood and shook his hand. "I'm Lincoln Davis."

"Come on back to my office so we can talk."

As I followed him down the hall to his office, I imagined that Frank was going to be my savior and help me get on the right path to making money and gaining independence from my family. He looked like the kind of guy who just knew shit that other people didn't know.

"Have a seat," he said, walking around to the chair behind his desk.

I sat down across from him.

"So talk to me. Ms. Allen up front told me that you just graduated and that this is your first time coming in."

"Yes, sir. But I'm eager to get out there into the workforce."

"Good. I'm sure you'll make us proud out there." He settled back into his chair. "So do you have a copy of your resume?"

"It's on my phone," I said.

He sighed. "In the future, it might be easier if you printed out a copy for us. In fact, if you want, you can email it to me right now and I can print it out. Here's my business card."

What was I thinking? I said to myself. I didn't want to get off on the wrong foot with this guy.

I sent my resume to his email address and waited as it came up on his computer monitor.

"Okay. I see it here." He paused to read it. "So you

have no prior work experience? Internships? Volunteering?"

"I didn't really have time," I said.

"Young brother, sometimes you have to *make* time for the important things." He continued reading. "Your cumulative GPA is a 2.3, and I see you have never had any academic distinctions or extracurricular activities." He took a deep breath. "What exactly *did* you do while you were here, if you don't mind my asking?"

I lowered my head. Outside of my father, I had never felt so judged. This guy was basically saying the same thing that Paris said yesterday, that I had fucked up a golden opportunity. "Classes, you know. It took me a while to find my passion. And you know, school didn't come easy for me."

"I have a learning disability, too. I'm dyslexic," he said. "We just have to work a little harder."

"Mr. Dole, I don't have a learning disability."

"Well, goddammit, man." He shook his head before adding an artificial smile to his lips. "We can still work with you. That's what we do. We help *all* of our graduates to get on their feet."

I could feel the "all" part of his statement stretching to fit people that he personally wouldn't have given much real consideration to helping, if he were employed elsewhere. If *my* job was, in any way, to help him do *his* job, then I had failed miserably. I started to stand up and leave, but I needed this situation to bear some kind of fruit, so I sucked it up.

"So do you have any idea of what type of employment you're seeking?" he asked.

I perked up. "Yes, I do. I'm looking for something in sports, entertainment, or law."

"What exactly do you want to do in those areas?"

"What do you mean?"

"Okay. Check this out. If Apple sent a recruiter to this campus for our annual job fair, which I'm guessing you didn't attend, they wouldn't just look for people who wanted to work for their company. They would be looking for people who were marketing a particular skill set that they might find useful."

I shrugged my shoulders. "I'm not sure I really understand."

"No problem. If you don't mind, take out your phone and do a search for job openings on their job page."

I did exactly what he said.

"Now look," he continued. "You'll see that there are a number of vacancies in different areas. Click on any one of them. Now you will see that each one has a set of qualifications listed under it. So if you walked up to a recruiter and said you wanted to work for them but you didn't know what job you were looking to apply for, they would ignore you. After all, it's not their job to look at your resume and scan through their database to find the perfect job that meets your qualifications. Now do you understand what I'm saying?"

I nodded. "I could do something with writing. My major was English."

"Good! Now we're getting somewhere. Let's look at the types of jobs that have writing as a major part of the qualifications."

We went through an enormous list of job titles, and he gave me some homework. I was supposed to select three of the titles that I felt I had the best matching qualifications for and come back later in the week to see what Ellison-Wright had in its database that corresponded.

"If you want, you just use your student ID and

password and access the portal on our website. You would be able to see exactly what it is that I see. I could then coach you on how to go about applying for —and hopefully interviewing for—the jobs you pick out. Deal?"

"Deal," I said, rising to shake his hand.

It hadn't gone as badly as it could have, but it was not as positive as I had envisioned it would be. I guessed this was what the real world was about, people not sprinkling roses on your shit, but instead giving you the truth, straight-up. Still, there was nothing that he asked me to do that I couldn't do. I was no longer alone in my quest for job. I now had someone backing me up.

I OPTED FOR A LATE LUNCH, that way I could eat one more time before I fell asleep. This time I opted for a combo at a burger joint in midtown. The burger was big enough to fill me up, and the fries had me to the point of being stuffed. I knew I would have to start eating better. At this rate, the junk food I was eating was going to catch up with me sooner than later.

I poured over my phone, looking at positions. After an hour it became clear that I was probably best suited for jobs anywhere between Communications Specialist and Technical Writer. My credentials were far from spot-on, but at least I wouldn't get laughed entirely out of the building. If only I could take another year to do an internship and get my grades up, I might be a more attractive candidate. My plan for the evening was to rework my resume so that it would be more appealing to HR managers looking to fill those positions.

As I put my tray away and topped off my soda, I

looked outside the window. Atlanta in May was a sight to behold, especially if you were in the midtown area. Skyscrapers pushed up in complementary patterns against a pure blue sky. It was the kind of visual that reminded you of a Solange song.

I walked block after block, my headphones nestled in my ears as I listened to KING's long-awaited debut LP, *We Are KING*. If my car were more reliable, I could have probably done some Uber driving. My old ride was best used for highway miles, not city miles, though. The plan was to drive it out to Duluth or Smyrna a few times a week, just to blow it out and keep the cobwebs from forming on the engine. I literally had duct tape wrapped around the alternator and had to ride around with the windows down to keep cool. I'm sure when my father bought the car sixteen years ago it was probably a woman magnet; now it was a woman repellant. You knew a car was jacked up if MARTA was the preferable alternative. But, truth be told, I actually enjoyed taking the train. Being from Mississippi, I didn't have the experience of riding a train—ever—so I grew to enjoy something as simple as zooming through the city on the transit affectionately referred to as Moving Africans Rapidly Through Atlanta. If you were in an area like midtown, however, a walk, especially on a sunny day, was ideal.

By the time I really took notice of where I was, I realized I was a few miles south of Piedmont. That's when I noticed this small bookstore, nestled between a record store and pizza parlor. Although I had been in Atlanta for six years, I had never seen this bookstore—and I had prided myself on staying up on things like that. I quickly crossed the parking lot to the store.

The sign above the store read "Nina's Nook" in a calligraphic font that danced across the illustration of a book. On the main window outside the store the words "Books and Other Dope Ephemera" blazed the eyes in a neon reddish electric script hung from inside. I smiled and pushed open the door.

The space was much larger on the inside than it appeared on the outside. With old Walt Whitman-like shelves lining the walls and inner aisles, a cafe in the back middle section, a table with jewelry and oils, and even a display rack of hand drawn greeting cards, the store clearly matched the description in the window. The place wasn't overflowing with customers, but there were more than a few people floating around, some in the cafe area, a few on small love seats scattered around the open spaces between tables and shelves, and others seated on the floor next to various shelves. The smooth, soulful sounds of Moonchild played softly in the background, a kind of dope Muzak to the whole scene. I immediately fell in love with the place.

On one of the front tables I found a copy of ZZ Packer's story collection *Drinking Coffee Elsewhere* and headed over to the cafe to sit down and read for a little while. I remembered reading one of the stories, "Brownies," in a fiction course I took a year earlier, so I got comfortable and spread the book open. I tried not to dwell on the fact that I couldn't afford to buy it.

I didn't know how long I had been reading when I felt something soft brush against the back of my neck and tickle me. I jumped, nearly knocking the book to the floor.

"Hey, you," Paris said. "How's the job search going?"

"Wow," I said, before I realized it. "I didn't expect to see you here."

She walked around and took a seat next to me at

the table. "I could easily say the same thing. This is one of my hangouts. I've never seen you in here before."

I smiled. "To be completely honest, I didn't even know this place was here until I walked in today. But now I don't want to leave."

"I feel you. Nina is dope, and this place is the shit." Paris placed the magazine in her hand down on the table. I quickly recognized it as *Wax Poetics*, an underground soul/hip-hop magazine for people who were serious heads. "So the job? Any news?"

"I went by the Career Placement office and met with a counselor. Things are starting to look up."

"That's what's up," she said. "Yo, did you put in an application here?"

My mouth fell open. I hadn't even considered working in a place like this. I was too caught up in the vibe for my mind to even go there. Hearing Paris say the words aloud pulled me back into the reality that I would really dig a work environment like this.

"By the look on your face, I'm guessing you haven't. Hold on. I'll be right back," Paris said, hopping up from the table and disappearing into the back of the bookstore. When she reappeared, she had a sheet of paper in her hand. "Here," she said, placing the application down in front of me. "It wouldn't hurt, right?"

"You are so deep inside my mind right now that it's scary," I said, pulling a pen from my pocket and going to work on the application.

While I filled in the information, Paris sat peacefully on her side of the table, pouring over her magazine, her curly twists resting easily over her shoulders, her cat-eyed purple glasses resting atop the bridge of her nose.

I finished the application and looked up. "I didn't know you wore glasses."

She reached over and took my application. "There are a lot of things you don't know about me." She smiled and walked away from the table again.

This time she re-appeared with a woman who bore a slight resemblance, except this new woman had a curly Afro and deep dimples in her cheeks when she smiled.

"Lincoln," the woman said. "I'm Nina. My sister just gave me this application and claims that I need to sit down and talk to you."

"Uh, yes," I responded, adjusting to this new revelation. "I was just telling Paris how much I loved this spot."

"Thank you. So do you have a minute?"

"Sure."

"Well, I'll catch up with you two later," Paris said, grabbing her magazine and walking away for good this time.

Nina sat down across from me, holding my application. "Just so you know, I don't really do this kind of thing—talking to people on the fly—but my little sister insisted I talk to you, so here we are."

She looked over the application and nodded.

"I have my resume on my phone, if you want to see it. To be honest, I just dropped in for the first time and had no idea I'd be applying for a job. Sorry I don't have anything printed out."

"Well, do you mind if I see your resume on your phone then?"

"No problem," I responded, pulling up the document and handing it over to her.

"So you just graduated. Ellison-Wright? Nice. English major, okay." She handed the phone back to me. "I only have a few questions for you."

"All right."

"Do you like to read?"

"Yes?"

"What's the last book you read that wasn't for school?"

"Honestly? Let me see. It's probably the *Ironheart* series by Brian Michael Bendis for Marvel comics."

"I see."

Fearing I was about to lose her, I added, "And before that, I read *Fledgling* by Octavia Butler—which is probably the best vampire novel I've ever read!"

Nina nodded. "I feel you. But you don't have to try to impress me. I'm a fan of little Miss RiRi Williams, too. I mean, who wouldn't be blown away by a fifteen year-old-sister who can build her own Iron Man outfit, right?"

I smiled. "True."

"Okay. My next question is are you a punctual and patient person?"

I nodded enthusiastically. "Yes, ma'am."

"You don't have to call me 'ma'am.' I'm not *that* old," she responded, smiling.

As I looked at her, I realized I could no more discern her age than I could Paris's. The only reason I used the word "ma'am" was because of her authority, not her age. But I didn't want to detour the interview explaining something that didn't really, to quote my mother, "have anything to do with the price of tea in China."

"If this is your first time in the store, I should probably tell you a little bit about what we do."

"Sure."

"As you can see, we're primarily a bookstore, but

we sell little odds and ends as well, mostly handmade items by local artists. There's also the cafe in the back, which, as you might imagine, really helps the bottom line. If I were to hire you, I would need for you to function in a number of different roles. You would need to help stock the shelves and tables, offer book suggestions to customers, be an occasional barista, and do a little cleaning up. I have a janitorial crew to come through and clean the store each night, but it's our job to keep the store looking good while it's actually open to customers. Feel me?"

"Yes."

"There are five us here, rotating various shifts, doing whatever is needed. You would make six. I'm pretty much here all the time."

"Cool."

"If you're interested, the job would be part-time at $10 an hour, but I could get you in some good hours every week."

"Sounds good."

"Well, the job is yours if you want it."

I thought about my conversation with Mr. Dole earlier in the day. From what I had read, to find a salaried job, it normally took a while. Even he couldn't give me a time frame for how long it would take to find one. Plus, a part-time job was good enough for me yesterday; why wouldn't it have been today? And then there was that "bird in a hand" metaphor. Honestly, though, I just loved the vibe in Nina's Nook and couldn't think of any place I'd rather be for several hours out of a day. There was also that Paris connection that placed a halo over everything.

"I definitely want the job," I said.

"Good. Can you start tomorrow at 10?"

"Absolutely."

FOUR

On the train back to West End, I couldn't stop thinking about the fact that I actually had a job. It might not have been impressive to a person who had a part-time job in high school, but for me, a guy who never held an actual job before, it was quite a huge deal. Plus, it gave me some leverage against my father for that imminent moment when the subject of my employment situation would come up.

I wasn't so naïve as to believe that one job at $10 an hour would solve all of my problems. It was just nice to know that I had at least one situation on lock. I would need employment elsewhere, too, but admittedly, it was easier to look for one job than it was two.

There was still the issue of my living situation. I could do another night on McCarthy's floor, but I would need to make getting out of there a priority. Part of me lay awake at night wondering if the Atlanta Police Department was going to kick in his door and drag all of us out of there for possession and intent to distribute. As far as I knew, weed was the only thing McCarthy had around, but Fulton County wasn't located in Nevada, Colorado, or California, so he couldn't afford to be sloppy.

My father, the righteous judge, would have me thrown in jail, just to teach me a lesson if I ever got caught up in some of McCarthy's foolishness, and it wouldn't have mattered to him one bit if it turned out I was innocent. "Don't hang around with knuckleheads" was one of his common bits of advice to me. But who didn't know at least a handful of knuckleheads? Hell, we had more than a handful in my extended family.

I picked up my phone and started making calls to friends. One by one, each of them told me that he was headed on to a grad program or job out of state, and the few who were remaining in the city were already on lock with their living situations and clueless as to who might be able to help me out, since they weren't able to. I could have said a lot about McCarthy, but when I really thought about it, he was willing to give me a place to sleep, even when my so-called friends played me to the side. Whatever became of my life going forward, I was determined to never forget this favor—assuming I didn't catch a case in the process.

I got back to the apartment to find the door locked and McCarthy incognegro. With the sun starting to set, there was no way I was going to just sit on the steps outside his crib waiting to "get got" by some local dude looking to test a college kid.

I dialed McCarthy and waited for him to answer.

"I can't come to the phone. You know what to do," his voicemail said.

"It's Link. I need to get into the crib. Hit me back to let me know when I can get in. Thanks."

It was probably better to head back to the MARTA station and shoot over to Buckhead until I heard back from him. I had no plan beyond that, only to check back in after an hour, if I hadn't heard from him.

As I rode the train back to the Lenox station, I thought about how serendipitous it was to run into Paris again. She was really starting to seep into my thoughts. I had tried to ignore it, but I couldn't get over how fly she was. Her skin was the color of hot chocolate, her twists the color of mahogany. The simplicity of her style left her beauty completely open and exposed, and that whole boho vibe she exuded made each little detail of her body that much more interesting, from the anklet that rested around one of her slender ankles to the soft, almost imperceptible absence of any nail polish on her fingers and toes. Every inch of her felt natural in a way that seemed entirely atypical of many of the girls I'd dated at Ellison-Wright. She was an earthy kind of woman, the kind that some knuckleheads would have referred to as a "granola girl." But then again Paris was also the kind of beautiful that obliterated the normal campus definition of the word.

Then there was the fact that she had been so damn cool. If it weren't for her, I would still be unemployed. I had run into her twice by accident. I was starting to get curious of what I might do if I ran into her a third time.

She was a mystery, but from everything I could glean from her, it was a mystery worth trying to solve.

I was so caught up in my thoughts, I nearly missed my stop. I stepped off the train with an hour left before the mall closed. I had no idea of what I would do to pass the time, so I walked down to the food court and stared at my phone, trying to resist the urge to mess around with my apps, since my battery power was below 50% and I still had to get in contact with McCarthy. In that moment I wished that I had Paris's phone number, just to talk to her and stave off the boredom.

I sat in the food court until the mall closed, and while I walked down Peachtree, my phone rang.

"Hello?"

"Nigga, I'm back. Had to handle some business. You can dip through whenever."

"A'ight."

I hung up my phone, and while a part of me was trying to be all cool and nonchalant on the phone, another part of me was both relieved to be headed back to the apartment, but afraid that the same situation could happen again and possibly for much longer.

I need to make getting my shit together a top priority.

WHEN I WOKE UP, I put all of my stuff into my bags and zipped them. With any luck I'd find a job and my stuff would already be packed for the move. I threw on a pair of khakis, a button-up with cuffed sleeves, and a pair of casual sneakers. Nina hadn't told me how I should dress, but from what I noticed while I was there, my clothes would fit in just fine.

I didn't have to report for another two hours, but I wanted to get acclimated with the area a bit better. Maybe there were other businesses around there that I had missed, too.

Nina's Nook was on a side of town that clearly sold fresh fruit, so I planned to eat there. In the meantime, I scanned my phone for people looking for roommates. Most of the ones I came across were for places that were a little too far out, either in distance or price range. Still, I was optimistic. The sun was starting to shine on me a little, and I felt that maybe my good luck was just beginning.

I grabbed an apple and a bottle of water from a convenience store and headed over to the block where the bookstore was. The record store, next door and physically in the same building structure, was just opening. I decided to walk in and take a look around. While the store had CDs throughout the front, it was clear the focus of the store was the massive used vinyl collection that filled out the remaining part of the store. As I perused the store, I wondered who would actually shop for vinyl records. Charge it to my youth. I didn't even buy CDs, so why would I buy something that would require an archaic machine to play it on. I couldn't even remember the last time I bought a full album of anything.

"Hey. You need help finding anything?" a tall brother with an even taller Afro asked, approaching me. His natty black t-shirt had the word "KUSO" scribbled across it, only adding to my confusion.

"I'm just looking," I responded. "Do people actually buy a lot of records in 2017? I'm seriously curious."

"Definitely. You wouldn't believe the comeback that vinyl has made."

"But what's the deal? My parents had a record player with a penny taped to the top of the part with the needle on it to keep it from skipping. I figure technology has evolved a bit since then."

"Yeah, but does technological evolution really kill off a good thing?. People still listen to the radio and watch TVs. Even with the Internet and smartphones."

I smiled. "It did for me. I cut the cord from cable and only watch Netflix and whatever is online."

The guy nodded. "You want to hear something?"

With nothing else going on, I said, "Sure."

He walked me over to a rather large set of speakers

and pulled up a chair. He had me sit down in the chair, spaced evenly between them.

"I know you're probably not an audiophile, but I want you to hear this song. This is on vinyl. I'm guessing you already know what a digital file sounds like on your iPhone, so listen to this with an open mind."

Earth, Wind & Fire's "Fantasy" started to pour out of the speakers, and I swore I could feel the thump of the percussion in my chest and the blares of horns sweeping past my face. I closed my eyes for a moment and it felt as if the band was standing only a few feet in front of me playing live. My head began to nod to the beat.

"You feeling that shit, huh?" the guy said.

"Yeah—but that's more of a testament to the quality of your speakers than the record."

He chuckled at this. "Dude, what you're hearing is an original edition of Earth, Wind & Fire's *All 'N All* album. You're hearing technology from the 1970s. It's not a testament to my speakers. It's a testament to Maurice White's amazing production abilities. He got all of this sound without the benefit of quantized beat machines and contemporary music technology. Even if you listen to this on your phone, you're not going to get a purer sound of this song than you're getting right now. This is not digital remastering. This is raw, in-your-face soul music."

As the music drew me in, I started to understand what the guy meant. I hadn't really given it much thought. Vinyl records were for hipsters, I had figured. Now I was seriously considering buying a turntable and picking up a few records to see if I could hear new things in the productions of other artists I liked. But I definitely didn't have discretionary income to be picking up new hobbies.

When the song finished, the guy asked, "So what did you think?"

I nodded. "I get it now. It's dope."

"So have a look around. If you see anything—or want to hear anything—just holler."

I shrugged. "Man, my ends are tighter than gnat booty. I just graduated and I'm trying to get situated with some employment first before I pick up any new toys."

"Did you see the sign in our window?"

"What sign?"

"The 'Help Wanted' sign."

"Guess I missed it."

He laughed. "Well, now you know. I'm Rob, by the way."

"Lincoln," I said, shaking his hand.

"Damn shame about Chester," he said, shaking his head.

I had remembered reading about the lead singer of Linkin Park in the news. "Yeah. That was a tough blow."

Why was there always the association of death with my name?

"I'd like to fill out an application, if that's cool."

Rob said, "No doubt. I'll grab one for you."

I had to laugh to myself at the odds that I might end up working next door to my new job.

As I filled out the application, I asked, "So what's KUSO?"

"It's a film by Flying Lotus."

"Who's Flying Lotus?"

"Dude, I so hope you get the job here, because I would love to put you up on so much stuff."

"Yeah, that would be cool." I really just wanted another job.

"Do you have a resume?" Rob asked.

"Can I email it to you? I have it on my phone."

"Sure. Just take one of our cards and send it to the email address right there," he said pointing. "Once my manager gets in, I'll give him your application. If he's interested, he'll call the number you left on the application."

"Cool. Good looking out."

I glanced at my watch, and with ten minutes left before I had to report, I sent my email to the record store while walking next door to Nina's Nook. The store was already open, so I walked in.

"A young brother who believes in being early," Nina said, smiling from the register counter. "You're off to a good start."

ALTHOUGH I HAD NEVER HAD a job before, I picked up on my duties pretty quickly. Most of what I had to do dealt with stocking the shelves, learning how to use the register system, ordering books that weren't already in stock, and just assisting customers in general. I wasn't given any responsibilities in the cafe, which suited me just fine since I didn't know the first thing about being a barista.

Because of the quiet lulls during the morning, I really got to familiarize myself with the layout of the store. By the time we got a run of people during the lunch hours, I was able to direct people fairly well to where it was they wanted to go.

While my job was not complicated, it gave me a sense of satisfaction that I was actually doing something to earn money for myself. That was the first step to being grown—self-sufficiency. When I finally got a break, I checked my phone to see if the record store had contacted me about interviews, but there was nothing there—yet.

Nina showed me the schedule that she wanted me to work, and it left a day or two open, where I could plug in another job with little problem, assuming they were willing to work with my existing schedule, something that I had not really considered.

The second big wave started rolling in around 4:45 and went strong up until 7. Friday nights were for open mics, Nina told me, so more than likely I would be needed on-hand to help out with that every other week. While I took this all in, I secretly hoped that Paris would walk through the door, but she never did.

As we were closing, I asked Nina if she knew where I might be able to rent a room on the cheap.

"I might know about something. Check back with me tomorrow when you come in."

"Great," I said. I hadn't expected much, but the possibility of a solution was encouraging.

"So," she said, "How do you know my sister?"

"We have a mutual friend. I actually just met her a few days ago."

"Well, she must think highly of you to recommend you for this job."

I smiled. "She's dope."

Nina smiled and nodded her head. "Yeah."

It seemed like she wanted to say more, but stopped herself. I wanted to ask more questions about Paris, but the conversation didn't really seem all that appropriate in the moment.

"I'm going to go ahead and lock up. You can log out of the system now. I'll see you in the morning."

"Sure thing," I responded.

After I stepped out of the store, I walked next door to the record shop. A large vinyl sticker of a vinyl record with the words Phat Daze Records stared at me from the glass outside the shop. It was still open, so I walked in to look around a little more—just in case I ended up getting a job there, too. Plus, I was in a mental state for memorizing layouts for stores.

"Dude," Rob said as I came through the door. "Pat is still checking out your resume and application."

"That's cool. I just wanted to stop by and look around some more."

"No doubt. So what type of music do you listen to?"

"Mainly old school stuff. My cousin loves 90s music, so he put me on to a lot of 90s hip-hop and stuff like that."

"That's was a good era," Rob said, nodding his head. "B.I.G., Pac, Nas, Jay Z, Wu-Tang, Tribe. Yeah. If you were gonna be a fan of any era of hip-hop, you could do far worse."

"True. True."

Just then I saw Paris walking past the record store, headed to Nina's Nook.

"Hey, Rob, I have to run, but I'll catch up with you later. Hopefully I'll hear back from your manager."

"A'ight. Be easy, dude."

I was almost in a full-blown run when I reached the sidewalk.

"Paris!" I called out.

She turned just before she opened the door. "Link, what's up?"

As I approached her, I realized that I didn't know what I wanted to say. I had been craving this moment for so many hours that my mind had simply failed to produce a plan should I actually see her.

"I just wanted to say thanks again for your help with the job. I just got off work a few minutes ago."

"Nice. So everything is working out?"

"Definitely." I paused to collect my thoughts. "Hey, I don't mean to be too straight-forward here, but can I get your phone number? Maybe we could grab a bite to celebrate the new job."

Paris took a moment to look me up and down and really take me in. It was an odd moment, this appraisal. Some of my boys loved to do this to girls walking down through campus, as they sat on the wall off the main strip. They referred to that strip as the "meat market." They did to girls what Paris was doing to me now, and it felt more uncomfortable than I had expected.

"So you wanna hang out?" she asked.

"Yes, I would like that."

"Do you have anything going on later this evening?"

"Not really. No."

"Well, hang around for a few minutes and let me holler at my sister. Then we can go kick it for a while."

"Sure," I responded.

She walked into the store, and I stood around on the sidewalk doing my best to look like I wasn't waiting eagerly for her to return. This was what I had wanted since the moment I saw her, and now my stomach began to fill with butterflies.

She was back before I was able to settle myself.

"How did you get here?" she asked. "Train? Car?"

"Train. I don't drive my car much."

"Why not?"

"It's an old beater. I don't have AC and it leaks oil like Exxon-Valdez."

She laughed. "You're a little young for that kind of reference."

In that moment I started to ask her age, but I didn't want to piss her off. I had heard that women don't want you to ask about their ages or weight —ever.

Instead, I responded, "I read a lot."

"Well, we can take my ride," she said, pointing to a dark gray colored crossover parked a short distance from us.

The car couldn't have been more than a year old, if that. It glowed beneath the street light in the center of the parking lot. She unlocked the doors, and I hopped into the passenger seat.

The inside smelled like the sweetness of her hair, coupled with some type of citrus blossom. I wanted to drown myself in the scent, it was so sexy. In that moment I asked myself, "What if she was that special someone, that prototype Andre 3000 had referenced on his *The Love Below* portion of that legendary Outkast album?" It was a huge jump from meeting her at McCarthy's crib, but it was one I didn't have much difficulty making—at least in my mind. I had only had one serious relationship during my time at Ellison-Wright, and that relationship with a girl named Jada had fizzled out when she had become more distant. Surely there was another guy, but she never admitted it. She just said that she didn't think it would work between us. I thought I would feel more hurt than I did, but I ended up using the breakup as an excuse to play the field, which wasn't all that it was cracked up to be. If I didn't take the situations seriously, there was no reason for those women to take them seriously either. I spent my "super" senior year just focusing on graduation. Playing the field that hard hadn't gained me anything, other than more time on a degree my father had grown tired of paying for.

"Nice ride," I said, checking her out behind the steering wheel. With The Internet playing loudly throughout the car, she had created a mellow environment, which seemed to be an extension of her style. I had yet to see her in an environment where she hadn't somehow transformed the feel of the room in some way.

"Thanks. You up for a ride?"

"Sure. What did you have in mind?" I asked.

"There'a this spot over off Cobb Parkway that we can eat at, down the street from my crib."

"I'm down."

As we hopped onto I-75 North, my mind raced with more questions about her. She had a nice car. Her sister owned a business. She lived in Cobb County. Was there more to her than her varied hustles? I was guessing so. But what? I couldn't piece together that part.

"So which of your jobs did you do today?" I asked jokingly.

"I worked on my novel and did a few hours at the consignment shop. Hold up. I love this part," she said, turning up the volume to the point that I had to almost place my hands over my ears. Syd's voice crooned smoothly over a spaced out track. It was a dope song, and her singing about her girlfriend put me in a space where I wanted to really make the most of this time with Paris.

"Whatchu know about The Internet?" she asked, moving her shoulders to the beat of the music.

"I know a little bit," I said, smiling. I might not have known who Flying Lotus was earlier in the day, but I knew The Internet. They were one of my favorite bands.

We listened to the song until it ended. She turned the volume back down to normal, and I leaned a little closer to her under the guise of wanting to be heard better, but the truth was that I just wanted to be closer to her.

"So is there someone special in your life?" I asked.

"Haven't we had this conversation before?"

"Not really. I had just asked what type of people you were drawn to."

She considered this. "Yeah. You're right. I'm not serious about anyone."

"So does that mean that you're single?"

"Pretty much."

None of her answers were straightforward, but I couldn't have cared less. I just wanted to be in her world in any way that she would allow me.

"What about you?" she asked. "You serious about anyone?"

"I can do you one better. I'm actually single."

She laughed, leaning forward in her seat.

"I'm a regular Chris Rock," I said, smiling.

"I don't think I've met a guy yet who doesn't have a piece of ass tucked away somewhere."

"Well, I can't say that I do. You should have caught me a year ago. Right now I'm just doing me."

"I feel you," she said. "That's really the best thing anyway. You don't want to be in some cornballl situation and then block someone who might be coming to you with the full package."

"That's it."

"You're an interesting brother."

"So that means you like me?"

"No doubt. We wouldn't be kicking it right now if

I didn't think you had a little *something something* going for yourself."

This made me smile. In the back of mind, I kept telling myself to be cool. The situation was mine to blow, if it were to get blown.

We arrived at a small restaurant called Liz's, yet another restaurant I had never visited during my exhaustingly long matriculation at Ellison-Wright. Being with Paris made me wonder just how much I didn't know about the city I was living in.

"Do you eat seafood?" she asked, parking the car.

"Definitely."

"The crab cakes here are slamming! Not all that filler, just great big pieces of lump crab meat."

I smiled, but in the back of my mind I wondered if I had bitten off more than I could chew. The first meal I paid for was barely $12 for the two of us. She was already talking about crab cakes, so I knew I could easily spend twice that amount on just her plate alone, not including gratuity. But I had a job, right? I'd get paid soon. Still, one of the lessons I did manage to learn from my father over the years was that it was not cool to spend money you didn't really have to spend. I could hear his voice in my ear as we walked into the restaurant, but I pushed it away because I had wanted everything with Paris in that moment to be perfect.

The server quickly seated us in a cozy booth near the back of the restaurant . The decor was the same kind of neo-soul flavor that permeated Nina's Nook, with African-American art prints on the walls, old school Shalamar piping through the speakers spaced out around the room. "A Night to Remember" played just above a whisper, and as I looked around the room, I saw a room full of black professionals nodding to the beat as they ate incredible looking dishes.

"I love this place," Paris said, doing a little old school dance from side to side, as she glanced briefly at the menu.

"I can get with this," I said, doing a little dance of my own.

"Oh, check you out! You got some rhythm."

I smiled. "I do a little *something something*."

"I see."

I looked down at the menu in front of me, the one page glaring back at me with prices that made my eyes water. At that moment I vowed to just bite the bullet on those $25 crab cakes and look at the evening as the celebration for my graduation, the one I never got from my parents. I would have as good a time as I could.

When the server arrived at the table, true to form, Paris ordered her crab cakes and a glass of wine. I ordered the same thing, opting for a Long Island iced tea instead of wine. If I was going to do it, dammit, I would do it the way I felt it should be done.

"So tell me about yourself," said Paris, her voice dancing over the top of Chaka Khan's "Ain't Nobody."

"I'm from a small town in Mississippi called Daily. I have a sister at Princeton. My father's a judge. My mom works for a nonprofit. I just finished school."

"So family is big to you. Cool. But I want to hear about *you*. Like, what makes you tick? What are you in to?"

"I just love to read. I got that from my mother. She works for a literacy foundation. I always wanted to be around books. I guess I never really gave it much thought, though—how to make a living from it. I just like doing it."

Paris nodded. "Maybe I'll let you see my novel one day," she said, chuckling. "Maybe."

"I'd love to read it."

"We'll see. So have you thought about working at a publishing company or something like that?"

"Not really. But I do have this dope job at a bookstore." I winked.

"Yeah. That's a good start."

"Definitely," I responded. "Okay, what about you? Tell me something about yourself."

"Well, you already know my hustles. Outside of that, I love writing. If I could make a living writing, that's what I would do. Bookstores are my sanctuary. Sometimes I drop by Nina's just to be in a space full of people who have successfully done what it is that I want to do."

"I can totally relate."

Paris leaned forward a little. "Something else about myself is that I'm sapiosexual."

"Sounds like some really freaky shit," I said, smiling.

She laughed. "It just means that I'm turned on by smart people."

The smile from my face dropped. "Damn."

"Why did you say that?"

"Hell, it took me six years to graduate with a 2.3 GPA."

"GPAs aren't everything, you know. I think sometimes people put too much emphasis on the wrong things. You can be smart and not make good grades. History is littered with people who weren't much for classrooms."

I nodded. "I guess you're right."

"I tell you what," she said, slyly. "If you tell me something that blows my mind at any point tonight, I'll give you a kiss."

A smile spread across my face faster than I could

stop. It was the first outward gesture that she might have been interested in me in an intimate sense. A part of me wanted to just start saying a flood of shit to her in hopes of finding a string of pasta that stuck to the wall, but the dominant part of me told me to be patient and look for an opportunity. Of course I thought about all of this without knowing if I could, in fact, say something that would impress her. I had to remind myself that I did score well on my college admissions test and that I had been reading voraciously most of my life, even if I didn't bother to work hard in my classes. That kiss was mine. I was going to will it into existence.

"I probably shouldn't have told you that," Paris said, eyeing me closely. "Now you're probably thinking about what you're gonna say. I don't want you not talk during dinner because you're so much inside of your head, so come here."

She beckoned me forward. I leaned forward.

"Come closer," she said.

I stood up a little and leaned in closer.

Paris stood slightly, closing the distance between us and placed her lips against mine. The softness and fullness of her lips pressed against mine felt almost magical. As I relished the feel of her, her tongue split my lips and danced playfully against mine. Once she finished, she cupped my chin in her hand and kissed me softly again, before siting down.

"We good?" she asked.

"Hell yes!"

"Good. Well, enjoy your crab cakes. They're on me."

FIVE

"So how are things working out with Mac?" Paris asked, polishing off her glass of wine. The crab cakes had long since been devoured, so we made ourselves at home nursing what was left of our beverages.

"Good as can be, I guess. As long as 5-0 doesn't kick in the door and take us all down to jail, I'm good."

She laughed. "You'll be fine. Mac is good people."

"I'll take your word for it, but I still need to find a new place. I'm serious about getting caught up in some deal gone awry."

"Mac doesn't deal. Hell, he smokes too much to do that. He just always has something on him. But trust me it ain't to sell." She set her glass to the side. "He has back issues from a car accident, so he lights up for the pain."

"It's still not legal in Georgia, though. Is it?"

"Only the oil—and that's for a handful of conditions, but it is what it is. People are gonna light up, just like folks in dry counties are gonna drink."

"Yeah, well my father would throw me under the jail."

Paris shrugged. "To each his own."

I suddenly felt like I might have come off as judgmental, so I started to backtrack. "I've always been curious, but at this point I can't afford to try anything and have my future employer test my cloudy piss."

"You might have a point."

"The other stuff aside, though, McCarthy really hooked me up by giving me a place to crash. It was either hit the floor at his crib or head back to Mississippi and pay $500 a month to live in the bedroom I grew up in."

"Damn. Your pops is for real."

"That's what I was telling you."

"Well, has Mac shown you any of his films since you've been there?"

I laughed hard before I realized that Paris was serious. "What? Like DVDs or something?"

"No. *His* films. The ones he made."

"McCarthy is a filmmaker?" I asked. Thinking back to my interactions with him, I realized that nothing about him screamed filmmaker—but then again, I didn't really know what a filmmaker was supposed to look like anyway.

"I'm actually producing a film for him."

I shook my head, completely incredulous. "Okay, I get it. You're joking, right?"

"I'm dead serious. He's shot a few short films—some of them were even official selections for film festivals—and he's still trying to get this latest project off the ground. When you dropped by the other day, we had just finished discussing some business. The kush was just a way to pay a sister for her time, since most of his funds are all tied up in the film."

I still couldn't believe my ears. If she was pulling a fast one on me, there was no way that I would've known.

"You should ask him yourself," she said. "He might even tell you what the film is about."

"Wow. McCarthy is a filmmaker. Who would have thunk it?"

"Thunk?"

"Hey, I'm from Mississippi. Give me some credit."

"Oh, okay," she said, smiling.

"So you're a film producer on top of everything else. You're a regular Jane-of-all-Trades. Is there anything you don't do?"

"Sure."

"Such as?"

"I don't play hockey—well, not ice hockey anyway. Maybe a little field hockey, though." She laughed.

"See?" I said, unable to conceal my amazement. "And you find *me* interesting?"

"It's not *things* that make a person interesting. It's that indescribable thing that draws me to a person, that *je ne sais quoi*. Either it's there or it isn't."

"Thank God I have some *je ne sais quoi* then," I responded, laughing.

"Yeah, you do." She laughed along with me. "So are you ready to head out?"

"Sure, but I have to be honest with you. I'm not ready to go back to McCarthy's yet."

Paris looked at her watch. "It's almost ten. If you want, we could head back to my place."

"Sure," I said.

I could still feel the kiss from earlier dancing across my lips. At that moment I would have followed her anywhere she wanted to go.

WE PULLED up to a gated community of townhouses

in a neighborhood tucked away off the main drive. By this time I was convinced there was a private map to metro Atlanta and that only certain people had access to it.

Paris opened the front door and immediately punched in her security code. She hit the lights as we walked into the foyer. Off to the side, in the den area, was a set of stylishly funky furniture in a Georgia red clay color, with what appeared to be original art canvases all around the walls. The hard wood floor was covered by what looked like a huge rug of a Basquiat painting. It was by far one of the dopest places I had ever been in—and it quietly begged the question "What did she do for a living that gave her a place like this?" Maybe I had misunderstood how much one could earn from working at a consignment shop or modeling for art students or singing rap hooks. But then her sister owned a business, so maybe that had something to do with it. I wanted to ask her, but money was even more taboo to discuss with a woman than age and weight, so I just put my curiosity on silence and followed as she showed me around the lower level of the townhouse.

"You live here by yourself?" I asked.

"Yeah. I've been here about three years."

"This place is incredible. It's like neo-soul/boho heaven in here."

"Thanks," she responded, kicking off her shoes in the hallway.

I did the same.

"Rent over here must be a beast," I said, taking in the ornate fixtures.

"I don't really know."

"You don't know?"

"I own my house, so I don't know what people are renting them for."

"Okay," I said, as we returned to the den and took a seat side by side on the couch. "What is it you're not telling me?"

"What do you mean?"

"I just feel like there is so much about you that I don't know."

Paris placed her feet under her bottom, and I felt myself staring at her full thighs beneath her tight jeans. "Then ask about what you want to know."

"You're cool with that?"

"Why wouldn't I be?"

"Well, okay. Do you own the consignment shop?"

"Yes, I do."

"And you own the bookstore with your sister and the restaurant?"

"No. The bookstore is my sister's and the restaurant is my aunt's."

"Okay."

"Are those all of your questions?"

"For now."

I felt like I had already been too intrusive, and for what? To find out something that I could've easily guessed.

"So it's my turn now," she said. "Why are you concerned about any of that?"

I shrugged my shoulders. "I guess I just want to know as much about you as I can."

"I'm surprised you didn't just google me."

"I don't even know your last name. But even if I did, I would rather get to know you directly. I'm not the type to cyberstalk someone I like."

Paris smiled. "That's a first. Most guys I know will

go search through your Instagram hoping to find a picture of you in a bathing suit or something."

"I'm not even on Instagram," I responded. "Should I set up an account?"

"No," Paris said, laughing.

"I would rather see your beauty up close and personal."

"I see."

I leaned closer to her, placing a hand on her lap. "I know this is going to sound strange, but can I hear one of those songs you sang a hook on? I am so curious to hear your voice over a rap track."

"You're crazy," she said, standing up and walking over to a speaker setup in her corner. She removed her phone and connected it to a 1/8-inch jack, scrolled through her iPhone screen, and then started a song.

As soon as the beat came on, I covered my mouth. "Oh shit!"

I had expected her to play some track from an up and coming rapper, someone selling mixtapes out the back of a hoopty, but this was Marz Banx, the legendary Afrofuturistic MC supreme.

"You like it?" she said.

"Hell, I *own* it! How did you get to do hooks for someone like Marz?"

"Mutual friends. I met him when I used to live in New York."

"Are you from there?" I asked.

"I went to school at NYU and met him through a producer friend of mine who was doing some work for Def Jam. We hit it off, and I did this track with him."

"Not to sound like a Stan, but he's my favorite MC, and knowing that's your voice on the track has elevated that song to my new theme song."

Paris laughed and returned to the couch.

"Wow," I said, looking at her again. "You are…perfect! I have no idea of how you came to be single, but I'll count that as my good fortune."

She looked at me emptily for a single moment, before her lips gradually spread into a smile and the warmth returned to her eyes. Then adjusting her legs, she placed her feet on my lap. "You don't mind, do you?"

"Not at all."

"Okay. So I have another question for you," she said. "If you were trapped on a deserted island for a week and only had one book with you, what would it be?"

"Hmm. Probably something I hadn't already read. I would want to be learning something new, even if I was on an island. Let me see. I'd probably go with this volume of Henry Dumas's stories called *Echo Tree*."

"Why him?"

"This dude was just dope. Poet, fiction writer, the works. And he was just getting started with his career before he got gunned down by a transit cop on some Oscar Grant shit. Mistaken identity, too. Toni Morrison was his editor. I think I'd want to read all of his short stories in a single volume, if I only had one choice. What about you?"

"I'd probably take *The Collected Poems of Lucille Clifton*. I just don't think I could ever get tired of reading her work."

"Good choice. I've read a few of her pieces. She's amazing."

"Yeah."

Once the song ended, the room became silent again, and I wanted desperately to say something smooth, but a yawn pushed its way up from the back of my throat.

"You tired?" Paris asked.

"Maybe just a little. I've been up since early this morning getting ready for my first day at the bookstore."

"Well, I'm glad that everything went well today."

"And tonight."

She smiled.

"Well, I should probably call an Uber. I didn't see any trains out here."

"What time to you have to be at work tomorrow?"

"Eleven."

"You can stay the night, if you'd like."

"I wouldn't be putting you out?"

"Nah."

"Thanks," I said.

I nodded my appreciation and followed her up the stairs.

<hr>

SHE SHOWED me to the guest room down the hall from her master bedroom. I was too tired to hope for anything other than a real bed to sleep on. By the time my head hit the pillow, I was out like breasts at Mardi Gras. Because I had been on the floor for the entire week, the softness of the mattress felt like a gift for which I would have gladly paid with my remaining savings.

Around three o'clock I woke up to the feeling of someone sitting down on the bed. I almost screamed out in the darkness, forgetting where I was.

"It's just me," Paris whispered, patting my back. "I couldn't sleep."

"You okay?" I managed through a veil of sleep.

"I was just wondering if I could lie beside you for a little while."

"Sure," I responded, turning toward her and wrapping her in my arms. She snuggled up against me, and like that, I went right back to sleep.

I WOKE up around 7:30 to the sounds of the local radio station's morning show and the smell of pancakes and juice. Again, I had to remind myself where I was.

Still dressed in my clothes from the day before, I walked into the guest bathroom and was relieved to find a small toothbrush, still in its plastic wrapper, and a travel-size tube of toothpaste. I quickly brushed my teeth and washed my face with the face cloth Paris had left for me.

When I made it downstairs, I noticed that Paris was already dressed in a radiant orange sundress, her hair pulled back into a ponytail, the twists having given way to curls. Everything about her looked beautiful, and I had to pinch myself at the fact that I had stayed the night in her house.

"Good morning," she said, her voice full of a cheer that I couldn't even begin to muster for at least another hour.

"Good morning."

"I made us breakfast. After we eat, I can drop you off at Mac's so you won't be late for work."

"Wow. Thanks," I said, taking a seat at the small glass table in her dining area. "I can't remember the last time I had a real breakfast—and that stuff they serve on campus doesn't count."

"It was the least I could do. I really appreciate you letting me sleep with you."

"Paris, those are the kinds of words than can make a man's ego uncontrollable," I joked.

"Ha ha," she said in exaggeration. "I sometimes have trouble sleeping at night." Her voice had become serious again.

"Well, I'm glad I could help."

I wanted to ask her why she had trouble sleeping, but I figured she would share that information with me when she was ready to.

We sat and enjoyed breakfast, and within the hour, she was dropping me off at McCarthy's so I could get ready for my day. I knew as she pulled off from the curb that seeing her leave would be the hardest part of my day.

SIX

"**N**igga. I almost put out a hood APB out on yo ass," McCarthy said, slouching in a t-shirt and sweats in his favorite chair, a vaporizer resting against his lips.

"My bad. I didn't know I was going to be out all night," I responded, curious as hell about why he cared at all.

"These streets are real, my nigga. If you gon' be out, just hit a nigga on the hip."

"Will do," I responded.

"So?" he said.

"So what?"

"Where was you at?"

His line of questioning caught me off guard so quickly that I actually blurted out an answer. "Paris's."

"Oh shit! Sit down, nigga. You got to spill it. Right now. You and P? My nigga, you gots to come up off that—right now."

I sat down. Part of me wanted to avoid any details at all, even though I knew nothing salacious had happened. Still, there was a part of me that was slightly touched that the dude whose crib I was crashing at was showing any real interested in my well being.

"We just got a bite to eat and went back to her place. We talked. I fell asleep. Nothing happened."

"You like her?" McCarthy asked.

I smiled and looked away.

"Yeah. You like her. Hell, you better like her if she letting you stay over and shit."

"I'm definitely feeling her."

"Be good to her, man. I'm serious. She good people."

It wasn't just McCarthy's words; it was the fact that he had actually referred to me as "man" and not "nigga." In the larger scheme of things it was a small thing, but with him it was immediately noticeable.

"I will," I responded. "She told me you're a filmmaker."

"Yep. Been at it now for almost ten years. Mostly just small films, but I got a feature I'm about to start working on."

"That's pretty cool."

He nodded, accepting the compliment.

"You want a hit of this?" he said, extending the vaporizer towards me.

"Nah. I'm good. I got to get ready for work."

"A'ight."

I rose from my seat on the couch and went over to my bag to get my things together. As I combed through the bag, I thought about the fact that I had just had my first real conversation with McCarthy. If Paris was an angel, it appeared that she sprinkled her magic on everything she touched.

I STARED at Old Steady Rock for a few minutes, reminiscing on a time when the car had been in its prime. I had used the car for two homecoming parades while I was in high school, had waxed it and used it in lieu of a limo on prom night, and had pulled onto the yard of Ellison-Wright as a freshman feeling like the shit. Somewhere between my fourth year and what would be my graduating year, the car's age started to show. I had taken it to a mechanic on the south side of Atlanta, and he told me that it would cost more than my car was worth to get the air conditioning fixed. When the battery started going out regularly, he wanted to charge me an arm and a leg for a new alternator. I doubt if my father even knew how jacked up my ride had become. He was already making me feel like shit for not finishing school on time, so I didn't bother to tell him. After the post-graduation ultimatum, I figured I had done right by not compounding my debt into his wallet.

To deal with the faulty wires around the alternator, I got a shade-tree mechanic to duct tape the hell out of it, holding the wires in place. I dealt with the air conditioning by keeping the windows rolled down, although in Atlanta, stopping at a light could make the car feel like a Lakota sweat lodge. As for the oil draining out, I just bought a few bottles of oil to keep on hand, along with some paper towels to check the dip stick every time I got into the car. Because my cash flow was so low, Steady Rock was on the bottom of my list of priorities. I still had a fondness for the car, though. There were too many memories in the front (and back) seat to just send her off to the vehicle graveyard.

I opened the door and scanned around to make sure nothing had been stripped from the car. I stopped locking the doors a while back after some crackhead broke out a window to steal a five dollar DVD. After that, I just stopped leaving things in the car and left the doors unlocked. I removed the radio from the car, and as long as I didn't have to pay for another window, I didn't really care if someone opened the door and went in the car, snooping around. I didn't even worry if anyone would steal the car or strip it down. They wouldn't get far, so the joke was on them.

I popped the hood and added some oil and checked the tires. They were worn down and needed to be replaced, but I wasn't about to give away the tires by leaving my vehicle parked in West End. I sat down in Steady Rock, my legs falling easily into the grooves of the old leather. I placed my feet on the clutch and break and started the car. The fact that I drove a stick-shift probably served as the biggest deterrent to anyone stealing it in the hood. I vowed that whatever my next car was would also be a manual transmission.

I rolled down the windows and pulled out the parking lot. Somewhere between my shower and my getting dressed, I had decided to drive to work. Maybe I just needed to feel in control of my transportation for the moment.

While hovering in the high eighties, the breeze from the windows was not as bad as I had expected. The drive was actually rather relaxing. I arrived half an hour before I was due to start work and parked in the back of the parking lot of the plaza. I pulled out my phone and looked at Paris's phone number. I had gotten it moments before she dropped me off this morning, but I had yet to use it. I was worried about coming off as too thirsty, so I decided to check my email instead. There was a message from Patrick Daughtery at Phat Daze Records asking if I would be available to interview for a the open position tomorrow morning at 9. I sent him a quick response that amounted to a "hell yes" and pushed send. Just then my phone rang.

"Hello?"

"Hey, Lincoln. How is everything going?"

I hadn't expected to hear my father's voice so soon. With a few days still left in the week, I figured I would call him on Sunday, if he didn't call me first.

"Everything is going all right," I responded. "I got a job at a bookstore, and I'll be interviewing for a job at a record store tomorrow."

"Impressive. I knew you could get a job if you put your mind to it."

I waited for him to tell me that I should have had a better source of income, given how much he spent on my degree, but he didn't.

"Hey," he continued, "You got a minute?"

"Yes, sir. I have to clock in in about fifteen minutes, but I have a few minutes."

"Well, I'll be brief. I've been talking to your mother about how we sprang that decision on you at the last minute. She thinks I should've given you a little more time to digest the news. After some careful reflection, I agree." He paused. "It's just that you're my only son, and I guess sometimes I put a lot of expectation on you for that. As a judge, I see a lot young men who make bad decisions. You've never been to jail. You haven't accidentally turned me into a grandfather. What I'm trying to say to you is that I'm proud of the man you've become."

I hadn't expected the tears to well up in my eyes, but there they were. "Thanks," I managed.

"So this is what your mother and I are proposing to you, if you're interested."

"Okay." It didn't matter what he was about to propose. I was just glad to be on his good side.

"I talked to one of my fraternity brothers in the admissions office over at State University, and he's agreed to hold a slot in the business school for you this fall and even help you to secure a fellowship. All you'd have to do is take the GMAT—and you know you're good at standardized tests. You could live at home—for free. We could even get you a new car, since I know that old one has been giving you some trouble. So what do you say?"

"Wow," I responded. I didn't even know what to make of it. My head was in the zone for my current job, not for what my father was recommending.

"So you take the test and score high on it, and I'll take care of the rest, okay?"

"Okay."

"How are you looking on money? I can transfer something over to your account this afternoon."

"Thanks, Dad."

"And where are you staying? You still at your friend's place?"

"Yes, sir."

"Well, what I put in your account should tide you over to the end of the month, and then your mother and I will drive up and pick up you and your things. Sound good?"

"Yeah, Dad."

"You don't sound all that excited."

"I guess I'm just getting ready for work."

"I understand. Well, we'll see you in a few weeks. Love you, son."

"Love you, too, Dad."

I knew I should have been happy that my father and mother saw it in their hearts to bail me out, but I couldn't get over a growing disappointment in myself. My father was already planning the next phase of my life—without me. He had gotten the last word, as he normally did, and as I stepped out of the car, I tried to ignore his offer as I headed to my second day of work.

SEVEN

My second day went as smoothly as my first. Rather than wait for something that needed my attention, I became proactive with doing my job and trying to anticipate what was needed next. With so much down time in a bookstore, it was either lounge or find something to stay engaged.

While straightening up a row of books in the reference section, I came across a preparation guide for the GMAT. I picked up the book and flipped through it. It had been a while since I'd had a math class, but I was always pretty decent at the subject. I took the book over to the counter by the register and worked a few problems. It wasn't that difficult. It was just the timing component of it. I figured with some practice I could probably get my speed up a lot and do solidly on the exam.

I returned the book to the shelf, mentally earmarking it as a purchase to make with my paycheck using the generous employee discount. I wasn't excited about leaving Atlanta, but I knew I had to at least prepare myself, if I didn't want to disappoint my father.

I got off around six and immediately called Paris.

"Hey you," she answered.

"Hi. How was your day?"

"Good. I definitely can't complain."

"I was wondering if you wanted to hang out again tonight," I said.

"Sure. What did you have in mind?"

"Anything. It's really about the company, not the event."

"That's what's up. Can you meet me at the Olympic Park by the fountains around 8?"

"Sure."

"Okay. I'll see you then."

After I hung up the phone, I walked next door to Phat Daze. I had a little time to spare and had decided that I would keep using Steady Rock for the rest of the day, so there was no need to drive back to McCarthy's. I would just need to check the oil again before I drove off—that and calling McCarthy to let him know I'd be out late again, more than likely.

"Dude, what's good?" Rob said, as I entered the store.

"Just chillin'. I work over at Nina's, and I just got off."

"I feel you. It's a nice spot over there. I don't read much though. Music is more my thing."

I nodded.

"So did you ever hear from Pat?" Rob asked.

"Yeah. He emailed me earlier today. I have an interview tomorrow."

"That's dope. You know he's here right now. I can go get him so you can at least meet him."

"Cool."

Rob walked off and returned in a few minutes with a large, heavyset bald guy with a thick beard. If he had been wearing shades, he would have looked like one of those flying monkeys from *The Wiz*. Without the glasses, he looked like the muppet version of Rick Ross.

"How's it going, Lincoln?" he asked, shaking my hand with the kind of grip that nearly bruised my shoulder.

"It's great," I responded, trying to match his enthusiasm.

"If you've got a minute, I can interview you now. I mean, you're here, and it's pretty slow in here."

"That's cool. I just got off work next door, so you'll have to excuse my appearance."

"Ha! That's rich. This is a record store. You're pretty dressed up by our standards. Come on back," he said, taking me through the doors into the back of the store.

BY THE TIME I parked and walked over to the fountains at Centennial Olympic Park, I was in full-blown celebration mode from the news that I had gotten a second job. There was a part of me that knew I should have turned down the job, especially if I was supposed to be leaving Atlanta at the end of the month, but I couldn't. Having never had a real job, I found it next to impossible to turn anything down, especially if I had applied for it.

For a week night, the city still hummed with activity, people enjoying the heat of late spring in a city that looked as if it were outlined in an orange halo. That was something that I had always liked about Atlanta: it was the kind of city that was beautiful year round.

Up ahead I saw Paris, her hair hanging loosely in a curly Afro, the brilliant lights of Atlanta behind her casting a surreal glow around her entire body. The light accentuated every curve of her body, and it took everything in me not to run to her and kiss her in a way that we had yet to explore.

"Hey you," she said, extending her arms to hug me.

I held her in my arms, smelling the sweetness of her hair. "I've been thinking about you all day."

"Oh really. And what have you been thinking?"

"This," I said, leaning in and kissing her. My heart beat wildly in my chest as she wrapped her arms around the back of my neck and stood on her toes to meet me.

After taking a comparative religion class in college, I had often wondered what heaven would be like to me, if I could construct one for myself. In that moment it became clear exactly what mine would be.

Once our lips parted at the realization we were standing in the midst of tourists and little kids, Paris smiled. "So we're really gonna do this?"

I nodded. "I can't see how we can avoid it."

She pulled me close to her again, kissing me deeply. "Well, let's head back to my place."

"I'm right behind you."

<hr>

AFTER ROLLING up the windows and parking Steady Rock next to Paris's crossover, we walked briskly into her townhouse. With the door still slamming shut behind us, she pulled me into her and resumed the magical kiss we had begun at the park.

We gradually worked our way through the foyer and up the stairs to her bedroom. With the lights still low, I was only able to make out the hugeness of her bed and the large sleigh frame that made the mattress look like a floating cloud.

I picked her up and placed her down gently on the

bed, lifting her sundress up, as I kissed down the insides of both of her legs. Her fingers danced across my head as I slid down her panties. Face-to-face with her moistness, I gently tugged at her lips, massaging her pearl, before sealing her in the warmth of my mouth and tasting her.

In the moments that followed, I lost track of time and space. The music surrounding me was composed of staccato breaths and moans, screams and random syllables of affirmation. When I finally entered her, it felt so amazing I questioned briefly if I had ever been with anyone before in my life. Her passion made everything feel brand new, and every lover I had ever had seemed to disappear into nothingness, as I lost my virginity all over again.

As we lay next to each other, our bodies drenched in sweat and post-climatic bliss, I whispered softly in her ear, "You are *amazing*."

"You're not so bad yourself," she responded, draping her leg over mine and kissing me gently on my chest.

Somewhere between listening to her breathe against my chest and staring at the ceiling fan, I drifted off into the best sleep of my life.

PARIS'S SCREAMS startled me from my sleep and I jolted forward, my eyes springing wide open in the darkness. I immediately scanned the room and realized that Paris was asleep next to me.

"Paris," I said, gently shaking her. "Baby, wake up. Wake up."

She screamed again before pushing up onto her elbows. "Oh," she said, before starting to cry.

I held her tightly and she squeezed me hard, sobbing softly into my chest. I rubbed her back, gently sweeping the hair back from her face.

Neither one of us said a word, but I stayed awake, caressing her back, prepared to rescue her from her dreams, should they bite back again. Pretty soon the deep breathes of her sleep resumed, but I held her closer.

———

I DIDN'T REALIZE I had fallen asleep until I awoke to Paris massaging my erection. Before I could speak, she climbed on top of me and welcomed me into a glorious morning, the sun filtering softly through the sheer drapes covering her windows.

When we finished, she leaned over and kissed me gently on my lips. "That was for last night," she said, before walking into the bathroom attached to her room and turning on the shower. "You're welcome to join me, if you'd like."

I followed her into the cloud of steam beginning to fill the bathroom. There we washed each other's bodies, exploring in the daylight what we had only felt during the night. My soapy hands glided over her smooth skin, and I ached to spend the entire day with her—like this—but I now had two jobs to prepare for.

Again we had pancakes and juice, and we kissed by the front door, before promising we would get together later in the evening.

I walked outside, checked my oil and added part of a bottle, before regretfully pulling out of the parking lot. As I drove toward West End, my thoughts turned to what had startled Paris so badly in her sleep. The lovemaking had almost made me forget about that incident, but now that my head was sobering, I began to wonder what had happened.

Two nights ago when she said that she couldn't sleep, she had crawled into bed next to me. Whatever it was, it was really doing a number on her. I wanted to be there for her in any way that she needed me. Still, I couldn't help wondering what it was that she was running from during the daytime that eventually caught up to her at night.

EIGHT

I called Mr. Dole over at the Career Placement office shortly before my shift at Phat Daze began. He congratulated me on my having found work and said that if I ever wanted to discuss employment strategies in the future to give him a call. I had little doubt that he wanted to help me, but I knew my getting a job helped to increase the percentage of recent grads finding work and that it was doubtful I would ever hear from him again. My name had likely been placed in the "closed" files, like some solved homicide.

I still hadn't heard anything from Nina about possible apartments, but I figured it made little sense to get into a lease when I would have to leave at the end of the month. While I welcomed the stability being offered by my father, I was starting to feel that I didn't really want to leave. Paris was a big part of that. Then there were the jobs—and beyond that, the possibilities of having a more interesting life than Daily, Mississippi, could offer.

I wanted to tell my father that I had changed my mind, that I wanted to stay in Atlanta, but I realized I had never *not* done what he had told me to do. Even though I was on the verge of turning twenty-four, I still feared telling my father "no" more than I did any-thing else. My behavior was a direct reflection of his teachings, as was my paranoia of failing his expecta-tions. Every time I thought about talking to him about the life I was creating for myself, I got sick to my stom-ach. During my first two years of college I suffered from irritable bowel syndrome as a direct result of my stress. Even with my diploma in hand, I didn't know if my poor performance in class was related to any of that stress.

My sister, Octavia, didn't have the same problems, though. Since Octavia was the youngest child, and the only girl in the family, my father preferred to en-courage her with adoration, while he felt my "being a young man" required criticism for the harsh world he felt I would one day have to navigate. My sister went to Princeton and was on the Dean's List; I went to Elli-son-Wright and barely graduated. I was raised to be-lieve my successes were the results of his teachings and my failures were all my own. I loved him and respected him, and I knew he wanted what was best for me, but sometimes I hated myself for being so dependent.

"DUDE, WELCOME ABOARD," Rob said, dapping me.

"Thanks. How long have you worked here?"

"About five years. I'm not going anywhere. I've never had a job that suited me as well as this one. Maybe one day I'll scrape up the money to buy it from Pat, if he ever decides to retire."

"Cool," I responded. "Is this the only business he owns?"

"Nah. Pat has his hands in everything. He's even a

part owner of a record label with a few cats from New York."

"Word?"

"Yep. They call it Trez To Be. It's like a funky take on the darkest planet in the universe."

"Is the label in Atlanta?"

"Yep. The dudes he runs it with went to Morehouse, so everything is set up here."

A part of me wondered why Rob didn't find the idea of working at a record label more attractive than working at a record store, but I was coming to learn that everyone had his own unique passion.

"We carry some of their music in here. It's actually pretty good. They mainly do alternative soul with a little rap thrown in the mix. They even did a track with Marz Banx a while back, so yeah, they're on the come up."

"Nice. I have a friend who recorded with Marz."

"For real? Dude is dope. Totally underrated as a top MC, but then so is Phonte from Little Brother."

"True."

Business was slow in the store, and I mainly used much of my time during my shift becoming acquainted with the inventory system, how all of the music was arranged, and who the key artists were in each of the categories we had labeled throughout the store. It wasn't all that different from what I was doing over at Nina's, but I figured that to be a good thing—at least for now.

With my father's deposit and two paychecks, I was going to be able to maneuver with a bit more latitude for the next two weeks. But after that, none of this would matter. I would have just been spinning my wheels.

By the time my shift ended, Rob and I had gotten

to be pretty cool with each other. He definitely helped the time pass by quickly. For the last hour of my shift, he and I talked about our favorite movie soundtracks. His was Spike Lee's *Do the Right Thing*. Mine was *New Jack City*. In the larger scheme of things, most people wouldn't have picked either of those soundtracks for even a top 100 list of movie soundtracks—and I think that's what helped us to hit it off so well. We just didn't seem to care what other people thought about our tastes.

After I left Phat Daze, I walked next door to Nina's. My shift there didn't start for another half hour, but I figured I would get something from the cafe and chill out until it was time to work.

As I sipped on my fruit tea and read through the GMAT preparation book I had set aside, I had flashes of the previous night. Imagining Paris's soft, shapely legs wrapped around my waist made me eager to fast forward through the next few hours to get to her again. During my break we had exchanged texts, and if the playfully suggestive nature of our words wasn't enough, she sent me a picture of her pulling her sleeveless t-shirt up over her bare stomach, her navel pierced and a Basquiat crown tattooed on her oblique with the words "To Repel Ghosts" beneath it. I hadn't really noticed it in the shower, but it was crystal clear in the picture. I had always found body art sexy, and she was delivering the type of image I was unable to stop fantasizing about.

"So how are you doing?" Nina asked, sitting down next to me. "I have to admit that it's pretty impressive that you always arrive early. That's a good trait to have."

"Well, I work next door now, too. I like being here, so I don't mind coming in and chilling before my shift starts."

"Okay," she responded. "You have a second to talk?"

I began scanning my mind to see if I had done anything wrong, maybe forgot to do something. I cautiously said, "Sure."

"My sister called me earlier today gushing over you."

A smile broke out across my face.

"Yeah," Nina continued. "I imagine she had that same look you have right now. So know this: I'm not trying to get up in your business and what not, but she is my only sister, so I've gotta know what your deal is with her. I can't let her get hurt, so if you're just toying with her, you need to come clean."

"I really like your sister. In fact, I think she's amazing."

Nina eyed me carefully, not quite skeptical, but not exactly full of joy either.

"I'm gonna be honest. I didn't know what to say when my sister started talking about you. What are you—22 or something?"

"I'll be 24 in three weeks."

"Yeah. My sister is not the kind of person to just mess around. She's been through a lot, and I don't wanna see her get hurt because you're young and don't know what you want out of life. You feel what I'm saying?"

I nodded. "Yeah. I understand. But I'm curious. You keep mentioning my age. I have no idea of how old Paris is, so I don't really know what you mean. All I can say is that I think the world of her and that I'm really looking forward to getting to know her even better."

"I see. Well, I'm gonna give you the benefit of the doubt and assume that everything is cool. And as long as you're cool with her, you're cool with me. But on the real, you guys should have serious talk about some things."

"All right," I responded, not having any clue as to what she was talking about, but sensing she was not going to share any more than she already had.

"Good. Feel free to log in when you get ready. I have to run to the bank this afternoon, so I'll be out for a few minutes."

"Thanks," I responded.

As she walked away from the table, I suddenly felt my stomach beginning to knot. The mysteries about Paris that I had tried to ignore were suddenly bubbling to the surface. With how I was beginning to feel about her, I knew we would need to have a real heart-to-heart. What was it that Nina—and even McCarthy—knew that no one was telling me?

NINE

Shortly before my shift ended, I received a call from Paris telling me to meet her at her apartment. Luckily I drove, so I quickly agreed. There was still a bit of concern from Nina's comments earlier, but it was starting to fade into the background as I began to fantasize about holding Paris in my arms again. She had awakened something in me that was intense, burning even.

After checking my oil level, I hopped on the highway, headed to Smyrna. Without a radio in my car, I was left only with the sounds of the road as Steady Rock raced up I-75 North. Once I reached the gate outside of her community, I buzzed her. After a few seconds, the gate slowly opened. I drove around to her building, having grown comfortable with the route by the third time.

When I reached the front door, Paris was already standing in the doorway, the candlelight so low inside of her townhouse that her body appeared as a banging-ass silhouette. I almost ran to her, I was so eager. As I got closer, I noticed she was wearing a dark blue silk kimono left slightly opened so that the laced chemise beneath it was visible. Other than that, she didn't appear to be wearing anything else. Her athletic legs looked even more appetizing when displayed against the contrasting color of the fabric. And her hair, that beautiful curly Afro from earlier, was pulled into a high ponytail, revealing the beautiful angles of her face. Her beauty was intoxicating. If I could have rewound time to take in the vision of her again for the first time, I would have.

"Hey you," she said, standing on the tips of her toes to kiss me. My arms slid easily around her waist, and I could feel the warmth and smoothness of her body through the silk.

"I've been waiting for you," she said, her fingernails sweeping ever so lightly across the back of my neck. Her tongue danced against my ear, as her breath tickled me, sending incredible chills down my neck.

"There is no place I'd rather be," I responded, lifting her from the floor so that her legs wrapped around my waist. My plan was to carry her to her bedroom, but we didn't make it there. Instead, we reached the stairs before her kisses pulled me down onto the steps. We made love right there at the base of the stairs as if the stairs themselves led up to heaven.

As we convulsed in ecstasy at the enormity of our shared orgasm, I felt as if I had somehow grown wings and could fly up to meet her on the penthouse floor of my dreams.

In the heat of all of that passion I had forgotten that I hadn't eaten dinner yet. My stomach growled a little, but I was determined to get more of this appetizer Paris was sharing with me before I pursued anything else.

She excused herself to go the bathroom upstairs, while I walked over to the half-bath downstairs. Looking into the mirror at the sheen of sweat on my chest and the reddish glow across my face, I smiled. So this was what pure happiness looked like.

When she returned, I walked her over to the couch and had her sit down. With her legs draped over my shoulders, we began round two. This time we stretched our lovemaking to tantric lengths, simply enjoying the fit of our bodies meshing together.

"I love the way you feel inside of me," she said softly, looking into my eyes.

"I don't want this to ever end," I breathed softly into her ear.

She pulled me closer, rotating her hips and lifting and lowering herself onto me.

Occasionally one of us would say something and the other would respond, and although I had never really talked to someone during sex, I found these light exchanges while our bodies moved in slow, fluid, focused movements to be even more intimate. We were completely aware of each other as we worked to please the other. If she had reached out to dap me in that moment, it would have felt as natural to me as breathing. Beneath the desire I felt for her was this denominator of genuine friendship and interest that I could only imagine was the foundation for any real, lasting relationship.

This time when we climaxed I was convinced we must have known each other in a former life or something. It was all so easy with her. I didn't have to try to impress her. She liked me for me. Although it had only been a week, I was prepared to let myself go completely.

Once we finished, she rose from me again, kissed me on my forehead and headed for the kitchen. "Want some water?"

"Sure," I said, rising to follow her.

We stood in the open refrigerator door for a moment, sharing a bottle of water.

"How do you feel?" she asked, smiling.

"As if I have been kissed by the universe."

"Wow. I must have really rocked your world," she said, chuckling softly.

"You couldn't tell?" I responded, laughing.

"That was *really* good," she said, as if she had just tasted a meal prepared by an Iron Chef and decided to abandon the pretense.

We returned to the den area and sat next to each other on the love seat perpendicular to the couch.

"Can I be honest with you?" I asked.

"Sure."

"I'm feeling some pretty strong feelings for you."

"I'd be lying if I didn't say that I felt the same."

"That's a relief." I paused for a second as I considered what Nina had mentioned earlier. "Please don't think I'm trying to pull us out of this mood, but I just wanted to know about what was bothering you in your sleep."

Paris looked away without responding.

"You don't have to talk about it, if you don't want to. I just figured since we were getting closer that maybe you could help me understand how I can better be there for you."

She slowly nodded. "I understand—and you're right. It's just so much."

"Well, let's start with some simple questions then, if you're up to it."

"Okay," she responded, slightly relieved.

"What is your last name?"

"Bennett."

"Really? That's cool. Okay, here's another one: how old are you? And before you answer, just know that I'm not trying to be disrespectful, but I was curious."

"Why are you curious?"

"You just seem to be on a whole different level with things than I am," I responded. "But you don't have to answer if you don't want to. I'm not trying to put you on Front Street like that."

She took a deep breath. "Thirty-six."

At first the words danced just above my awareness. It was as if my mind couldn't reconcile what it was hearing with what it was seeing. Nothing in Paris's appearance suggested she was even north of twenty-five. She was clearly destined to be beautiful well into her eighties in the Lena Horne and Eartha Kitt sense. I smiled at the idea of us years from now, faces still glowing. I admired the life she had created for herself, and while my desire for her ran deeply, there was a huge part of me that wanted to live up to her expectations of me as well. I hoped that my own age and inexperience didn't threaten what we were experiencing.

"Does my age bother you?" she asked in the wake of my silence.

"I have to be honest. I wasn't expecting it, but it's not a big deal."

"You sure? I know it's gotta be affecting you at least a little bit. I have to admit your age concerned me a little bit when we first started talking, but I decided to just wait and see where things went."

"I'm all in, if you are," I responded, placing my hand on top of hers.

She smiled and my heart melted like a chocolate bar on the dashboard of a car in July.

"So can you tell me about these nightmares?" I asked, wanting to know more about her.

"You really want to know?"

"At this point we should probably get everything out there, if we're serious about seeing where this goes."

"Okay." She took a long, slow breath. "Five years ago I was engaged."

As the words entered into the still space between us, the candles still flickering around us, I suddenly felt that what she was about to tell me was going to be disturbing and that once it was spoken into that space things would change a little bit between us. Still, I had to know.

"Well," she continued. "We were three months away from the wedding. All of the invitations had been sent out, the caterers had received their deposits, I had finalized my dress, everything was in order. Damon, my fiancé, had already purchased the tickets for our honeymoon in Honolulu. He was a good man. He loved me and I loved him." She stopped talking and took a deep breath.

"He left you at the altar," I said, in an effort to help her get the story out.

"No. He killed himself."

For a moment neither of us said anything. The words were so heavy they silenced us, and that thing I had been fearing was now resting right there between the two of us.

"It was a Wednesday. He walked into the Marriott Marquis around lunch time and took the elevator to the forty-seventh floor. He jumped from the interior balcony in the atrium." She paused. "For months I blamed myself. Maybe I had put too much pressure on him or accidentally said the wrong thing to trigger him. His uncle later told me that Damon had always suffered from severe depression, but I had never seen him going through it during the two years we were together. Learning about his depression after the fact was a surprise, and it took me a while to believe that I had nothing to do with what happened. In my dreams I see him going up the elevator. Just as he is about to jump, I scream for him to stop. Then he falls."

I searched for words but was completely dumfounded. I couldn't even begin to imagine dreaming of my fiancée committing suicide every time I went to sleep.

"So I started seeing a therapist," Paris said. "I've made a lot of progress. But if I'm gonna be honest with you, you're the first person I've been serious about since it happened."

"Wow," I finally managed. Suddenly everything between us intensified tenfold. I was so intoxicated from the sex that I had not even considered that there could be anything heavier in the background. Suddenly I felt the need to tell her about my father and what he was proposing.

I cleared my throat. "I have to tell you something, too. My father called me and told me that he got a connection of his at State University to admit me to the business school there. He and my mother are coming to pick me and my things up and take me back to Mississippi in two weeks."

"What?"

"I'm supposed to be going to business school."

"I heard that part. You're leaving? In two weeks? When were you gonna tell me?"

"I was still trying to figure things out."

"So you just wanted to fuck me before you left?"

"No, it's not like that," I said.

"You know what? Get the fuck out of my house."

"Hold up. It's not like that. I really care for you."

"Lincoln, I'm not playing with you. If you don't get the fuck out of my house, I'm calling the cops."

"That's not fair. The cops? Come on. I really care about you."

"Lincoln."

I stood up slowly and grabbed my clothes from the floor. As I dressed, I continued to plead my case.

"I don't want to go to Mississippi. He's forcing me to. It's not my fault."

"Grow the fuck up!" she screamed. "Get out of my house!"

I walked to the door, afraid to look back at her crying face, the candles flickering against the wall reminding me of the tenderness we had shared only moments earlier. I started to speak again, but didn't want to press my luck. I closed the door clumsily behind me and walked to my car.

Why did I say that? I'm so stupid, I thought.

I sat down in my car and cranked it. I didn't want to leave, but I had no choice. I glanced at the time on the dashboard. It was a few minutes after midnight, and I was on the wrong side of Paris's door.

I reluctantly backed out of the parking lot and left the gated community. Within minutes I was on I-285 West, headed back to McCarthy's apartment, Old Steady Rock speeding past the endless black wall of trees that obscured the lights of Atlanta. As I replayed everything that had just happened, large droplets of rain began to splash randomly against the windshield. Then the bottom fell completely out of the sky and it seemed as though I had driven underwater.

A few miles from my exit onto I-20 East, I felt Steady Rock begin to sputter, and I remembered I had forgotten to check the oil level before I left Paris's. I had been too distracted.

Steady Rock, please don't fail me now.

I slowly pulled over on the shoulder, just as my car

gasped its last breath and smoke wafted up through the thick sheet of rain.

I grabbed the steering wheel and screamed my lungs out.

The cliché "when it rains, it pours" came to mind and only pissed me off further.

Fuck!

TEN

"Man, you owe me. Got me getting up in the middle of the night to scoop your ass up," McCarthy said, before adding "Nigga."

"I know," I said, leaning my head against the window.

"And don't get that fucking wave pomade all over my shit over there."

I sat up in my seat. "I really fucked things up with Paris."

"Dude, I told you that you couldn't do that. That girl has been through too much for you to mess with her mind."

"I know. I wasn't trying to."

I expected him to pull over and dump me back off in the rain. Instead, he said, "Tell me what happened."

So for the remaining fifteen minutes of our drive back to West End, with the rain beginning to clear, I told him what had happened and how I had tried to walk back the harm that I had caused.

"Yeah," he responded. "You really fucked that up. And when were you gonna tell me you were heading back to Mississippi? Dude, your communication skills are sorely lacking."

"I know."

Once we returned to the apartment, McCarthy said, "Get cleaned up and get some sleep. We can talk about this shit in the morning."

"So you'll help me?"

"Help you with what?"

"To get Paris back?"

"Dude, from what you just told me, I'm not convinced you even deserve a woman like her."

"You're probably right."

"But you should still fight for her, if you believe you can be what she deserves."

"Thanks," I responded.

"Don't thank me yet. From where I stand, you have Kilimanjaro in front of your ass."

STILL RESTLESS, I found it nearly impossible to go to sleep. When I finally passed out, I had a dream. In the dream, I was standing in my home in Daily, talking to my father.

"I'm returning to Atlanta," I declared.

"In what? You killed your car because you didn't take care of it."

"I'll catch a bus."

"And what're you going to do when you get there, Lincoln? Huh? Work at a bookstore and a record store? That's the best you can do with a $140,000 education? Maybe we should've let you take out student loans so you could see how long it would take to pay back an amount like that with minimum wage. As expensive as your education was, you would've had to take out private loans, and there's no loan forgiveness for those just because you can't find a real job."

"Well, I'm thankful to you and Mom that I don't have to consider that. I just want to live a life that makes me happy."

"And what's that?"

"I want to work where I want to work. And I want to be with Paris."

"Paris? That thirty-six-year-old woman you were talking about? You're barely an adult. Why would you want to strap yourself down with a woman twelve years older than you? Her biological clock is so loud I can hear it all the way from Atlanta. You can't even take care of your own self. How could you manage a relationship like that? Plus, when you're thirty, she'll be 42, and, son, it only gets worse from there. Can't you date someone closer to your own age?"

"Dad, I believe that I might be falling in love with her."

"Well, you've already messed up that relationship beyond repair."

"But I can fix it."

Then my dream cut abruptly to me standing on the sidewalk in front of the Marriott Marquis. In front of me, Paris walked into the lobby, so I followed her. She approached the atrium looking around, before her eyes finally found an elevator moving upward, the glass revealing a figure I could barely make out from the distance.

The dream jump-cut again to the inside of the elevator. Once it reached the forty-seventh floor, I stepped off. I looked around for the man I had seen moments earlier.

It's time to fly, I could feel my mind telling me. I walked over to the interior balcony. From there, the first floor looked miles away. My legs became weak. I placed my hands on the rail, believing that I was pushing myself away from it, but my legs jerked forward.

I could hear Paris's screaming from below. Then I was falling—fast.

My dream did another jump-cut. This time I was standing in a dark room surrounded by my father, Nina, McCarthy, and Rob. They chanted in unison, "You can't save her. You can't save her. You can't save her."

Then I was standing in the center of the fountains at Centennial Olympic Park.

"You're getting all wet," Paris said, giggling and pointing at me.

I swept my hand, shooting droplets of water onto her. "And now you are, too."

Her smile was so radiant that I couldn't resist walking to her and kissing her. It felt magical.

"Life is complicated," she said, apropos of nothing.

"Yeah. I know."

"You have to figure out what's important to you and follow through."

"Well, you're important to me," I responded.

"Am I?"

"Of course."

"I don't need you to save me. I just need you to be there for me."

"I know—and I will."

"Are you sure?"

Then she was gone.

"Paris! Paris!" I yelled. "Where are you? I can't see you." And then I said, "I love you."

Everything went black, and when I could see again, McCarthy was standing over me. "How can you love a woman you've only known for a week? Nigga please."

Then I woke up.

WHEN I AWOKE, I lay there on my back staring at the ceiling for several minutes before sitting up. The dream was still racing through my head, but with each passing second it was fading. By the time I stood to my feet, the only real thing I could remember about it was that I needed to talk to my father. Everything started and stopped with him. If I was going to make sense of my life and what I wanted for myself, it would start with me talking to my father and being truthful about what I wanted, whether he liked it or not. He was right when he had said that I had graduated out of his pocket. I needed to stand on my own. I needed to be my own man, even if that meant I would fall on my face from time to time. I needed the chance to do me.

I picked up my cell phone and dialed his number.

"Good morning, Lincoln," he answered.

"Good morning, Dad." I took a deep breath. "There's something I need to tell you."

"Is everything all right?"

"Yes, Dad, but I'm not coming home and I'm not going to business school."

"What do you mean you're not going to business school? You know how many strings I pulled for you to get in? I used up a favor for you."

"I appreciate that, Dad. I really do. But I didn't ask you to do any of this for me. After you and Mom left, I began to do things on my own. And, yeah, I'm a long way from figuring everything out, but I'm making progress. And I don't want to leave. I'm staying in Atlanta."

"Are you sure about this?"

"More than anything."

"Well, let me tell you a few things, son. I'm not

your enemy. I have never been your enemy. I have just been trying to get you ready for the time when you would be able to stand on your own in a world that wrestles with its feelings for black men. Yes, I was tough on you. As your father, I had that responsibility. I would have been derelict in my duty if I didn't do my best to prepare you for a world that doesn't care about your feelings.

"I've been a judge for twenty years, and was a prosecutor for ten years before that. Do you know how many black men have come through my courts?"

"No, Dad. I don't."

"Legions, son. Legions. After a while seeing young black men who look like my own son coming in and out of my courtroom can do something to you. I have tried to help as many of them as I could, because I know some of my colleagues on the bench can dispense sentences unjustly—throw the book at a black man and slap a white man on the wrist for the exact same thing. Well, I can't be the judge of everything you'll experience in this world, so I had to get you ready so that you could stand strong if the world chose to treat you like an 'other.' It was all out of love."

My eyes began to water. "I know, Dad. And I know I haven't always made the best decisions, but I had to try to do things on my own. I appreciate the safety net you have given me, but I just need to find my own way now."

"It's hard for me, son. Believe me."

"I know, Dad. But you have to just trust that what you and Mom taught me over the years took hold. And I know that it did."

"So you're really going to stay in Atlanta."

"Yes, Dad."

"You know I've known you your entire life, so I

understand that you have two jobs now. But there's more to it than just that, isn't it?"

I smiled, wiping my eyes. "Yeah. Her name is Paris."

"Does she make you happy?"

"Really happy, Dad."

"Well, if you're happy, then I'm happy. I didn't ask you for your input when I started courting your mother back in the day, so you don't need my permission to follow your heart. Do you understand what I'm saying?"

"Yes, Dad. And thank you."

"Any time." I could feel him smiling into the phone—just like me. "And Lincoln?"

"Yes."

"I love you, son."

"I love you, too, Dad."

Before I hung up the phone, I quickly added, "And Dad, I might need your help. Steady Rock has gone on to that great Mercedes graveyard in the sky."

"I'm actually surprised that she lasted as long as she did," he said laughing.

I started laughing, too, lightly at first and then with my entire body.

"Okay. We'll see about getting you another car. We can work on that *together*. Cool?"

"Absolutely," I said, unable to wipe the smile from my face.

I called Paris but she didn't answer, so I hung up and sent her a text message that said, "I'm sorry about last night. Please call me. I have something to tell you."

Once I put my phone down, I walked over to the couch and sat down. McCarthy had already left the apartment. I started to turn on the television, but the silence of the room helped to calm my thoughts. I didn't know if Paris would call me back, but I was going to keep trying to get her attention—at least until she gave me a chance to better explain myself.

The only place I had to be today was Phat Daze, and that wasn't until later in the afternoon. This was the only day—other than Sunday—that I had a free day at Nina's Nook. That suited me just fine because I wasn't eager to get chewed out by Nina over how things went down with her sister. I just needed a little more time to fix things.

Now that I would be staying in Atlanta, the search for a place to stay was back on. I wondered if maybe Rob knew anybody who needed a roommate. Truth be told, I had actually grown to appreciate McCarthy a lot more, and if he didn't have a one-bedroom apartment, I would have easily approached him about rooming together. As fond as I was becoming of his place, I knew there was no way I could continue living out of a suitcase and sleeping on the floor. It wasn't even a matter of pride. It was a matter of practicality.

I showered, got dressed, and walked down the street to the MARTA station. One of the things I had come to appreciate about taking the train was that I could avoid the wild driving in the twelve lanes of traffic of downtown Atlanta. I could also ride in an air conditioned environment, which was almost a requirement for summer travel in "Hotlanta." Mississippi was much simpler. Fewer lanes, and everything was close enough that you were never in the car long enough to sweat.

As I sat down on the train, I considered that I'd spent six years at school and had not established friendships that proved as valuable as the ones I was creating in the week after graduation. I had no idea of what my life would look like when my fellow graduates reconvened at homecoming in October. That was still a ways off, and I had no idea of where my head would be.

I enjoyed my jobs, but I was also aware that Congress was trying to take away affordable health care and that I needed to get a job with benefits. That would be an issue for another day. Right now, though, I just wanted to do well at my current jobs.

I got off at my stop and walked several blocks to the plaza. I was early again, but it didn't really matter to me. I knew Rob would be there, and he loved to talk about music and movies. There wasn't a better way to pass the time, as far as I was concerned.

When I entered the store I saw a group of guys at the counter by the register talking and laughing with Pat. They all had that glow that black men with real money tend to have. Rob was standing nearby and beckoned me over.

"Link, those were the dudes I was telling you about. The dudes from New York who own the other part of the record label."

"Cool."

"You know him?"

"Who?"

"Cool Brown. The dude over there," he said, nodding his head in their direction.

"No. I meant it was cool that—never mind." I looked over at the guys again and realized that Rob seemed a bit more concerned about them than I did.

"I think Pat's gonna shut down the store and go with the record label full-time."

"Oh," I responded. I hadn't even been an employee for a week and now there was talk of closing the shop down? "How do you know?" I asked.

"I've just been floating around picking up snatches of things here and there. I think Cool and J came down to talk to Pat about expanding the label."

"Well, who's the other dude?" I said, pointing at the fourth guy, a diesel dude standing by the counter wearing a Marvel Black Panther t-shirt.

"I don't know who he is, but he came in with Cool and J."

"Well, my father always said not to worry until you have something to worry about," I said.

"Ha! That's actually not bad advice."

"So what else has been going on around here?" I asked.

"Same old thing—but that's a good thing."

"I feel you."

I started helping Rob sort the stack of vinyls he had brought up from the back of the store. I figured keeping our hands busy would shut down the anxiety I could tell he was starting to feel.

"Hey, Rob. Let me holler at you for a sec!" Pat called out.

"Here we go," Rob whispered to me. He followed Pat, Cool, and J into the office at the back of the store.

Technically my shift hadn't started, but I walked over to the guy at the register with the Black Panther shirt on.

"Need any help?" I offered.

"I'm good."

"Hey, that's a dope t-shirt."

"You a Black Panther fan?" he asked.

"Yeah, from way back—long before the movie."

"Me, too. Glad to see Wakanda on the big screen, though."

I nodded. "Maybe now we'll see Miles Morales and Riri Williams up there next."

"You up on Marvel like that?"

"Definitely. Before I went to college I was pretty deep into comic books. I've only stayed up on a few of them over the past few years, though. Classes started kicking my ass."

He laughed. "Where'd you go to school?"

"Ellison-Wright."

"Word? That's my alma mater, too!"

We dapped each other, and it was like a veil came down between us.

"I actually graduated last week."

"Well, congrats, man. And you're working here?"

"Yeah. I'm grindin'. This is only my second day."

He shook his head. "Well, that's some pretty interesting timing."

I started to ask him what he meant, but I already knew.

"What was your major?" he asked.

"English."

"Really? What did you plan to do with that—before you got the job here?"

"I don't really know. I was starting to give some thought to working at a publishing house, maybe. A friend of mine told me I should consider it."

He smiled, nodding his head. "I'm an editor for a graphic novel publisher."

"Really? Which one?"

"Cool Empire Press—over in Little Five Points."

"Whoa!" I said. "I know about them. They're right up there with Image."

He nodded. "Something like that. So what's your name?"

"Lincoln Davis."

"I'm Chucky Buckner."

"Good to meet you."

"Same here."

The door to the back office opened and the four guys emerged. I immediately looked at Rob to see if he was all right. He had a goofy smile on his face, so I took it that the news wasn't as bad as he'd expected. Maybe the store wasn't shutting down after all.

"You good, son?" J said to Rob, nudging him playfully.

"Yeah. I'm pretty good. My head is still spinning."

"What happened?" I asked to no one in particular.

"Your boy is gonna come work for us at our record label here in Atlanta."

"Oh," I said, suddenly realizing that I had just been fired. "Congrats, Rob."

"Thanks, man," he said, his face still dazed.

I couldn't really tell if he was happy or not, but he definitely seemed to be digesting the news well.

"Lincoln, let me holler at you for a sec," Pat said, nodding toward his office.

I followed him back, but this time it was just the two of us.

He took a seat behind his desk and pointed at the chair in front of him for me to sit down.

"Hey, man. I'm gonna be honest. I didn't know things were gonna to work out like this with my label. Those guys out there, Cool and J, they just helped us to score a distribution deal, and I'm gonna have to shut the store down to focus all my energies on this new direction."

I nodded slowly, giving him time to tell me about how I would move over to the label with Rob.

"I know I put you in a funky situation, so I can pay you for the next two weeks, but this will be your last day."

I dropped my head. I wanted to be mad, to have a reaction, but what did I have to really be mad about? I'd only been there for two days. Still, the situation felt niggerish as shit.

Now I was down to one job—and that one job was dangling by a thread because of my stupidity with Paris.

"Thanks," I offered, rising from my seat. "I appreciate you giving me a chance anyway."

As I turned to walk away, Pat said, "Lincoln?"

"Yes."

"Man, keep your head up. As we grow the label some more, who knows? I might just give you a call."

"Yeah," I said.

As I walked up through the store toward the exit, my head hanging down a little, I could see Rob look at me with an apologetic look.

"Nice meeting you all," I offered, trying to lift my head as high as I could to show some dignity.

I walked out of the store into the blazing hot sun of Atlanta. I had nowhere to go and nowhere to be—and no idea of what to do next.

TWELVE

The first time I saw Atlanta, I could hardly believe I'd be able to function in a place so *big*. Daily, Mississippi, was a small town, the kind of place you might see in old Faulknerian depictions of the South. The Humma County Courthouse was literally at the center of a downtown square, where it was guarded on all four corners by the statues of Confederate soldiers who all seemed to be standing guard for the stainless banner embedded in our state flag.

Race relations were decent, but outside of a few wiggers, most white people socialized away from black people. Sure, black people were represented in the local government, but there had never been a black mayor. In Daily, it always seemed to be a race of races.

Atlanta was different, though. Although my parents talked about it from time to time, I could see for myself that the city was a Mecca for black professionals. It made me feel good that a major American city could be black like that: a black mayor, black congressmen, black fire chief, black chief of police, black man's name on the airport, blackity black black black. I felt like Allen Payne's character from *CB4*. "I'm black y'all! I'm blacker than black and I'm black y'all!" And after navigating the politics of race in Daily for eighteen years, Atlanta was my reward.

Every section of the city seemed to have its own flavor. If you were driving down Peachtree Street, you could turn off on any street and it lead you to some hidden neighborhood with an entirely different vibe. It was the kind of place where you could envision living there after you had graduated. By the time I graduated, I couldn't imagine down-sizing my expectations to fit Daily again. I had outgrown it. And my parents knew this.

As I walked down the street, the enormity of the city threatened to engulf me. Who was I in the larger scope of this metro area of nearly six million people? No one really had a reason to care about what I did or didn't do.

I took a seat on one of the walls lining the sidewalk and collected my thoughts. Self-doubt was a mother-fucker, and I knew I needed to take a moment and stop it right there.

I took a few deep breaths to clear my head. *What do I do?*

At that moment someone drove past me, windows down, playing Outkast's "Elevators," a song that seemed to encapsulate the group's desire to rise up in the rap industry, while grinding it out on a level where most rappers were just trying to make a living. I could hear the bass drops and the sounds of the guitar, and my mind started to drift.

I thought about all of the people who had started out with little or nothing, but made it to the top of their game, all right here in Atlanta. Maybe that would be my story.

No. It *would* be my story.

I remembered my first conversation with Paris

where she told me to be careful about what I put out into the universe. I had to be deliberate in my desire to excel.

I looked around, taking in the huge sunlit skyscrapers. I refused to just float through the next few years of my life. I had a choice of who I wanted to be —just like Big Boi said in the Outkast song "Liberation"—and, dammit, that's what I was going to do.

I decided to continue walking down to The Underground and promptly headed over to the Five Points MARTA station.

There was no doubt in my mind where I was headed next.

I HAD BEEN SITTING in the lobby so long that I could feel my ass going numb. Occasionally the receptionist would look in my direction and shrug, her way of letting me know that she didn't control the rhythm and flow of employees moving throughout the floor. I smiled and nodded. The fact that she even let me in without an appointment made me grateful to her.

Large pictures lined the walls, most of them panels from different issues, but the main feature of the lobby was the neon sign of the Cool Empire Press logo, centered where anyone getting off the elevator could see it.

I didn't know if Chucky Buckner was coming back to the office today or not, but I knew I had to at least try. The address had been easy to pull from the Internet, and while I could have easily explored the other businesses in the neighborhood of Little Five Points, I didn't want to chance missing him.

The receptionist waved at me, and I looked up.

"You can leave a message with me. I'll be sure to give it to him. I know you've been waiting for a while."

"I appreciate it," I responded. "I think I'll wait just a little longer, though."

"All right."

I looked at the assortment of comic books on the table in front of me. I had been tempted to read a few, but I wanted to keep my mind focused and felt that I might get distracted if I lost myself in one of the stories.

I glanced at my watch and saw that it was approaching 4:30. Maybe he really *was* out for the rest of the day. It made sense that he wouldn't be coming back if his friends from New York were in town. I had rolled the dice on his being here, but crapped out.

I could always come back another day and try this again. Still, something in me was riding off of a momentum that needed to be followed. I just needed to be patient.

I stood up slowly and stretched my legs. As I rotated my ankles, the door from the stairwell in the corner opened and out came Chucky.

My heartbeat tripled, and I tried desperately to remember what it was that I wanted to say. It was like I had amnesia and could barely remember my name. I took a deep breath and said, "Mr. Buckner?"

He looked up just as he was about to walk past me.

"Hey! You're the guy from the record store. Len… Lincoln, right?"

"Yes." I extended my hand, and he dapped me. "Do you have a minute. I just needed to talk to you."

He considered this for a moment and responded, "Sure. I have a few minutes. Come on back with me."

As I walked behind him, I mouthed the words "thank you" to the receptionist and headed through the secured doors into a maze of cubicles. I followed Chucky around to an office in the back of the room, one on the corner of the building with a view of the neighborhood, in all of its beautiful Bohemian funkiness. He pulled the door closed behind us and took a seat at his desk.

"So what's up?" he asked, pointing to the chair on my side of the desk.

While I didn't want to sit down again—since I'd been sitting for so long—I wanted to be as respectful as possible.

"I just wanted to connect again."

He leaned back in his seat. "So what did Pat say to you back there at Phat Daze?"

"Just that he had to let me go. I should've seen it coming. I was just kind of hoping that he might've needed some more help over at the label. But that's not why I'm here," I said.

He smiled. "Then why are you here?"

"Because I can be the best assistant that you've ever had. I majored in English and have a solid knowledge of the Cool Empire catalog and comic books in general. I'll get coffee. I'll make copies. I'll do whatever it is I have to do to learn this business and be the support you need as you continue to rise through the ranks." The words fell out of my mouth so quickly that I had to take a moment to breathe once I finished.

"I like your energy, but what makes you think I need an assistant?" he responded.

"With all due respect, Mr. Buckner, you don't *need* an assistant. It's like Joe Clark said in *Lean On Me*, 'I don't have to do nothing but stay black and die.' But what I'm offering you is a chance to have the *best* assistant, a person who is willing to do what it takes to have your back. I know I don't have any experience in publishing, but I'm a quick study. I know I can do this for you. All you have to do is give me the chance."

"I don't know. This is not how we go about hiring people here," he said, leaning forward just a little in his chair.

"I understand. I don't normally pop up at people's places of employment to see if I could get just a few minutes of their time either. I'm here because I know I have a lot to offer you and this company. I'm hungry. No task is too small or too big. I'm just asking for the chance."

Chucky leaned back in his chair again. "You know, Lincoln, this is not the easiest industry for people of color. As you probably know, most of the people in this industry don't look like me or you. Most of the books published in this industry don't reflect us either. Make a storm trooper black and people lose their minds. The indigenous people always need to be saved by the white man. It's not an easy industry to thrive in, but I've been able to do that for several years now.

"You say you are hungry, but I need to know that you can stay hungry, because if you can't, you won't last —whether it's with us here or some other company. You understand what I'm saying?"

"Yes, sir," I responded.

"Just call me Chucky."

"Yes, Chucky."

"So what am I saying then?"

"You're saying that I need to stay hungry."

Chucky laughed. "Yeah, I'm saying that, but I'm also saying I can talk to the editor-in-chief about bringing on an assistant editor, if you're serious."

"I can't get any more serious."

"Okay. Well, let me check out a few things. I'm not making any promises, but I'll fly it up the flag pole to see if anyone salutes it. Shoot me your resume and references and we'll see what happens."

I jumped from my seat and shook Chucky's hand. "You won't regret this."

He smiled. "I know. I better not."

THIRTEEN

I headed back to McCarthy's to give him the good news. When I arrived, I saw him dressed in a button-up shirt and khakis sitting in his favorite chair. Seated across from him on the couch was another guy dressed in a polo shirt and jeans. They were laughing when I entered the apartment.

"What's good, Link?" McCarthy said. He pointed at the guy on the couch. "This is Troy Dobbs. He's an Ellison-Wright alum, too. He does movies out in L.A."

I walked over and dapped him. "Nice to meet you."

McCarthy continued. "He's agreed to executive produce the film for Paris and me."

"Wow! That's great news!"

"Exactly. Your girl's on the way over right now to go over some stuff with us."

I nodded my head slowly. "Okay. I can get out of your hair for a while, if you need me to."

"Nah, man. I'm not kicking you out or anything. Just giving you a heads-up, that's all."

"Thanks."

Shifting gears, Troy asked, "So when did you finish up at Ellison-Wright?"

"A week ago," I said.

"Nice. I'm in town for my twentieth anniversary. This knucklehead here just had his tenth anniversary."

"What? McCarthy, I didn't even know you went to Ellison-Wright! Why didn't you ever tell me?"

"Thought you knew. My bad."

"So when you let me crash here, you were doing it because we were both alums?"

"Hey, man, I've been where you are. That's what we're supposed to do. Look out for each other and whatnot."

It had not occurred to me until that moment that being a graduate of Ellison-Wright had certain benefits. I had never expected to be a part of any of the alumni connections that people sometimes bragged about. I had assumed that there were cliques that looked after each other, but this wasn't a clique. These were people genuinely interested in helping me. I had not run into so many graduates of my alma mater in a single day since the commencement.

"So Link, not trying to put your business out there, but Troy knows a little bit about getting into complicated relationships with women after graduation."

Troy nodded, smiling. "Yeah. We all get swept up. Maybe it's the newness of being turned loose in the real world."

"Yeah, Link has it bad for Paris."

The conversation had turned so open that I didn't even have time to get embarrassed about this stranger knowing my situation.

"She's a little older than you, isn't she?" Troy asked.

"Yeah," I responded, reluctantly.

"Dude, don't sweat it. Same thing happened to me. At the end of the day, age is just a number. Compatibility is the real issue. Are you guys compatible?"

"I think so."

"Yeah, they are," McCarthy said. "He's got some smoothing over to do, though. This guy made the mistake of telling her he was leaving town right when she was starting to get close to him."

Troy shook his head. "I don't get it, man. In this age of connectivity, why do relationships have to end just because you move. I carried out a long-distance relationship with my ex for three years, Brooklyn to Los Angeles. You can't get any farther away from someone than that. And all we had was email and phone calls."

"I'm not leaving, though. Not now." I looked over at McCarthy. "That's what I wanted to tell you. I'm working on getting a job over at Cool Empire Press. I just met with Chucky Buckner a few minutes ago."

"Word!" he said, dapping me. "I know Chucky. We go way back. I'll be sure to put in a good word for you. So you're staying?"

"Definitely."

"So maybe you can help me with this rent on this new place I'm getting over in midtown, that is if you still need a roommate."

I laughed. "I still need to make sure that the job goes through, but you can count me in."

"Good luck to you, Link," Troy offered.

"Thanks."

"Now we just have to get you cleared up with Paris, right?" McCarthy said. "Hope you got some knee pads. You gon' have to do some Keith Sweat-level begging."

"I'll do you one better. I'm prepared to go Lenny Williams with my shit," I said, laughing. "Oh-oh-oh-oh-oh-oh-oh!"

Troy laughed. "He's got the right idea."

"That's that Ellison-Wright man in him," Mc-Carthy said between laughs.

BY THE TIME PARIS ARRIVED, I was sitting on the steps that led up to the second floor of the building. Because McCarthy lived on the second floor, she would have to walk right past me to get to her meeting. In the moments before she arrived, I worried if sitting on those steps was too much of a stalking move. McCarthy was all for it. Troy wasn't sure if it would work. I simply figured that it couldn't hurt—but now that I was on the steps watching her emerge from her car, I was seriously second-guessing myself.

"Really?" she said the moment she saw me. "You can't give it a rest, can you?"

"Hey, I know you have to talk to McCarthy and Troy, but I just need for you to hear me out for five minutes. I promise. I just need to talk to you."

She sighed and rolled her eyes. "Five minutes. No more."

I rose from the step and offered it to her to sit while I stood facing her. "First, let me apologize for the other night. I didn't mean for everything to go down the way it did. Up until I opened my stupid mouth, we were having one of the most amazing evenings of my life."

Paris looked away from me for a moment. I couldn't tell what she was thinking, but I continued, "I called my father back and told him I wasn't leaving Atlanta. I'm going to stay."

Paris faced me, her expression difficult to read.

"And," I said, "I'm working on getting this new job. Something full-time. That means I might have to talk to your sister about my hours." I had hoped the last part might elicit at least a smile, but it didn't. "It's just that there was a lot of stuff that we shared with each other, and I wasn't smart in what I said. Hey, I haven't had feelings this strong for someone before, and I let some things come out of my mouth that I shouldn't have."

Paris responded, "So you would have kept me in the dark about what you and your father had planned?"

"No. I would have just stood up to him sooner so it wouldn't have been an issue at all for us." I paused and reached for her hand. She extended it to me. "I'm not perfect, but make no mistake that my feelings for you are genuine. I want to be there for you. I want to give us a chance to see where this goes."

Paris continued to hold my hand as she spoke. "I know I put a lot on you pretty fast. Most men would have run away as soon as I gave them a glimpse of what you've seen so far. I guess, in my head, I figured that it would be better to not even allow myself to get any more wrapped up in you than I already had. I don't want to be hurt again."

"And I don't want to hurt you."

"But you can't always control that. Life does what it's gonna do. Things happen."

I nodded. "True. But I feel we owe it to ourselves to see if this chemistry that we share is the real deal. It sure as hell feels like it could be—at least to me."

Paris looked down for a moment. "Maybe I moved too fast with you."

"I believe we did what we did because we both felt there was something special between us. Let's not second-guess what our hearts are telling us."

Paris chuckled. "You have an answer for everything, don't you?"

"I just want to make sure I put it all out there before you go up those steps."

"Well, can we talk about this later? I mean, I have a meeting right now."

"Definitely. Just call me when you have some free time, and I will meet you somewhere so we can talk."

Paris released my hand. "I can't believe I'm actually considering this."

I stepped up onto the step just beneath hers. "Consider *this*," I said, leaning in to place a kiss upon her waiting lips. It was the kind of kiss that I knew I would replay in my mind years from now.

"So we're really gonna do this?" Paris said.

"I believe I've heard those words before, and the answer is still an enthusiastic yes."

She smiled at me, before turning to walk upstairs.

"Hold up. One more thing," I said.

She turned to face me. "All right."

"But, soft! what light through yonder window breaks? It is the east, and Paris is the sun. Arise, fair sun, and kill the envious moon—"

"What are you doing?" she asked.

"Trying to use a little Shakespeare to score some *sapiosexual* points."

"Boy, you're crazy," she said, stepping down and kissing me, before walking back up the stairs.

I stood there for a moment, listening to her knocking on the door and then entering the apartment.

I walked down the sidewalk toward the train station. A smile tickled the edges of my lips, and I tried to imagine what my life would be like tomorrow. I didn't really know. Things were always changing—and proving to be far more unexpected than I had imagined. Still, there was Paris and the promise of what our relationship held, and, for me, that was enough to comfortably face whatever tomorrow would bring.

ACKNOWLEDGMENTS

I would like to thank Torrey Holbrook Walker, Sabin Prentis, and Nikki Holbrook-Williams for all of their help with this book. I truly appreciate each of you and thank you for your time and support.

I would also like to offer a very special thanks to Nia Forrester, a wonderful writer and friend. Your advice and encouragement mean a great deal to me, and I am glad you were able to help me fine tune this book.

Thank you to Dr. Lloren Foster, who was my mentor and friend. He supported me in countless ways over our ten-year friendship. Words cannot express how much I will truly miss him.

Finally, I would like to thank my wife, Lauren, for having my back (sides and front, too) through this entire journey. I know it's not easy being married to a writer, but you handle that burden far better than I could have ever hoped.

ALSO BY RAN WALKER

<u>The B-Sides Books</u>

B-Sides and Remixes

30 Love: A Novel

Afro Nerd in Love: A Novella

<u>The Mississippi Books</u>

Mojo's Guitar: A Novel (Il était une fois Morris Jones)

The Race of Races: A Novel

<u>The Black/White Project</u>

Black Hand Side: Stories

White Pages: A Novel

<u>Other Books</u>

Bessie, Bop, or Bach: Collected Stories

Four Floors (with Sabin Prentis)

The Keys of My Soul: A Novel

The Illest: A Novella

ABOUT THE AUTHOR

Ran Walker earned his Bachelor of Arts in English from Morehouse College and holds a Master of Science in Publishing from Pace University and a Juris Doctor degree from George Washington University Law School. He has worked for several magazines, including *The New Yorker*, *American Heritage*, *American Legacy*, *Vibe*, and *Spin*. After leaving publishing, he returned to his home state of Mississippi and practiced law, before yielding to his true calling of writing. He is currently an Assistant Professor of English and Creative Writing at Hampton University in Virginia.

Ran is the recipient of a 2005 artist grant from the Mississippi Arts Commission and National Endowment for the Arts and an Artist Mini-Grant in 2006, and he has also served as an Artist-in-Residence with the Commission. Ran is a past participant in the Hurston-Wright Writers Week Workshop and is the recipient of a fellowship from the Callaloo Writers Workshop. He is the author of twelve books, and his short stories and poetry have appeared in a variety of anthologies.

He lives in Virginia with his wife and daughter.